CODE 1990

A catalogue record for this work is available from the National Library of Australia

CODE 1990

RAY KEIPERT

ALSO BY RAY KEIPERT

Life's Winners and a Few Losers

Five in the Quiver

A Hand of Aces

' ...People will rejoice. They will rejoice before you as
people rejoice at the harvest... For you will break the
yoke of their slavery. And lift the heavy burden from
their shoulders.'
– Isaiah 9: 3-4 (NLT)

'Freedom is never dear at any price. It is the breath of
life. What would a man not pay for living?'
– Mahatma Gandhi

'Ask not what your country can do for you, but ask
what you can do for your country.'
– John F. Kennedy

On a personal note, I dedicate this book to readers and friends who sadly passed away before having the opportunity to read it. One was Hermione who willingly allowed me to use her Christian name for one of the characters who, like her, had a great love of horses.

Next, with one of the great struggles of our time being that between dictatorship and true democracy, *Code 1990* is dedicated to many unnamed brave individuals. These are people who courageously defend the cause of personal freedom over an autocratic state, in extreme cases being forced to take up arms to valiantly repel a ruthless invader.

Finally, I gratefully acknowledge those who stand for honest elections over sham voting procedures and citizens who believe in truly representative government. May the present era of dictators cementing themselves into lifetime positions of power soon be destroyed by the will of the people declaring an end to repression. It can't come soon enough.

FOREWORD

Welcome to *Code 1990*, Ray Keipert's first published novel. This follows three books of short stories produced earlier this decade. Ray tells me that his first novel from the mid-1970s remains unpublished, although not without merit, and some themes from that work are used throughout this one. This simply proves creative writing can live again!

Ray is heartily opposed to dictatorship or autocracy and believes fervently in democracy and the rule of law. You will find this theme in abundance in *Code 1990*. While this book is a work of fiction, it is based on some real historical events. However, the threats posed by the autocratic, espionage-based regime highlighted here were all too real and, if anything, could be seen as understated. It may be years before the truth of this becomes entirely evident.

Intrigued? Well, delve into this two-part novel. It begins with the closing phase of the war in Europe and progresses through the Cold War all the way to... no, I won't spoil it for you. As you read, all will be revealed and you may well ask yourself: Have I ever known people like those portrayed here? Who knows, the answer may surprise you. I trust you will be gripped by the plot and characters of *Code 1990*.

Norm Hawkes
Past President of Myall University of the Third Age and fellow writer

PART ONE

CHAPTER ONE

They had long suspected this horrible place was here, surely one of dozens similar. Yet now they had rushed to the location as liberators, it was an absolute shock to every sense the human body possessed.

First the smell hit. The whole complex was foul, with the fetid stench of decay and death all around.

'Man, it stinks to high heaven!' one of the first to gain access impulsively yelled out. Others nodded in agreement, blocking their nostrils against the noxious odour from decaying corpses. Cowardly Nazi guards, intent only on fleeing to save their own skins, had left them in piles, unburied. Well over ten thousand corpses, scattered around. The smell was disgusting, gut-wrenching and utterly pervasive. An affront to humanity.

'Help us, we have no food! Please – we beg you! Please…!' Those inmates barely clinging to life were frantic, and there were uncounted numbers of them. Their plaintive pleas echoed down the lines of the barbed-wire compounds.

Poor wretches.

Other piteous cries of the starving prisoners assaulted their ears. Nor could they look away from the sight of those desperate creatures, dressed in the filthy rags of what remained of their camp uniforms, hanging off their skeletal bodies in tatters.

Their liberators hesitated to touch anything they didn't have to, wary of contact with typhus, lice or other contagions. As for the final sense, taste, many incoming British soldiers from the Eleventh Armoured Division would quietly fall out to find a private spot and spit out the bile that they'd brought up in response to the ongoing horror. They'd never seen anything like it and hoped never to do so again.

Bergen-Belsen concentration camp. A monument to man's inhumanity to man.

The officer overseeing one area of the campsite's Allied occupation, First Lieutenant Benjamin Fletcher, ordered his troops to assemble for instructions and receive a careful plan of action involving bringing relief to the unfortunate inmates as soon as possible. They needed a few quiet moments to assess the situation before beginning the marathon task, and he willingly gave them exactly that. He thus had a little time to reflect on the military campaign which had brought him to this spot in Northern Germany. Yes, his initial thoughts took him back about a month, to that stage of the Nazi retreat and his exultant shout out...

'On the home stretch now – we've got Jerry on the run!'

His mates gave thumbs-ups all round. A supporting artillery salvo confirmed it.

Just past the middle of March 1945, Benjamin Fletcher felt the long campaign was at last coming to an end. The British Army's military operation to finish this drawn-out war by crossing the Rhine River in the north, heading towards the enemy capital of Berlin, had begun. They and their American allies in the US Ninth Army took the lead in this massive thrust into the heart of Germany. The US First Army was in action as well, using its firepower to great effect.

'Keep heading east, we'll wedge 'em against the Red Army. It'll soon be over!'

The young officer's optimism was justified. The British Second Army moved straight across the extent of the North German plain, reaching two rivers, the Ems and Weser, in early April.

Next task – liberate the notorious Bergen-Belsen concentration camp in Lower Saxony, near the city of Celle. A blessing for the soldiers or a curse? Target date: April 15. They made it right on cue.

There it was, right ahead.

On the orders of General Montgomery, Ben and a large number of other officers and troops were detached from the Second Army, tasked with freeing the unfortunates imprisoned there, then with cleaning up, managing and eventually eliminating the camp. A challenging but essential requirement. Being a compassionate man, once he'd thought through his new mission, Ben was happy to obey.

So here he was. A veritable labour of Hercules before him. Not just huge, it was monumental. A count would give well over fifty thousand half-starved prisoners and many thousands of corpses, left in the open to rot.

Clearly, the priority in his allocated area was with the living, those poor skeletons of human beings whose meagre rations had deteriorated even further during the recent harsh winter. Finding food, decent sustenance with vitamin supplements, was absolutely urgent, so after the brief break, it was now time to thrust his troops into action. Ben set about this challenge with all the strength he could muster, using platoons of soldiers to scour nearby towns and villages for whatever could be found. They would brook no resistance from the populace.

With that effort underway, he turned to the matter of a burial for the many deceased inmates who hadn't lived to see the liberation. First, the piles of corpses. Then those unfortunate prisoners, too weak to respond to first-aid treatment, who had since died.

Ben spoke enough German to make himself understood.

'Right, Fritz – form a work detail and get ready to start the burial!' was his order to the guards who hadn't managed to escape. They complied, awaiting instructions.

Once bulldozers were available, the British soldiers dug vast holes to form mass graves and the conscripted Nazis were ordered to dispose of the many dead. It revolted them, but their conquerors were past caring about that. It would take as long as it needed. The British would work their new captives around the clock. Union rules out the window!

An enlisted man approached Ben with a complaint. The Nazi conscripts were rough-handling the dead still in piles. Calling a meeting with the Germans, Ben emphasised '*mit Respekt*' as he pointed to the dead and with a sweep of his arm indicated the large pit before them. They got the message, and his soldiers supervised a more respectful burial.

As he turned to leave, he noticed a slight twitch in the arm of a body on top of one pile. 'What the heck?' Yes, there was another. 'He's still alive! Soldiers, come over here – call an orderly! This one's not dead yet!'

True enough, there were signs of life, but the poor man was pretty far gone.

'Get him to the infirmary!' The makeshift hospital the British troops had now set up in Ben's area of the camp site. 'And check the others for any signs of life.' They did so meticulously, but the man Ben had chanced to notice was the only one found still alive, though barely.

Later, after spending some time supervising the burial procedure was back in operation, Ben checked on the man now in the infirmary. Miraculously, he was beginning to stir. Ben wondered if one of the vicious Nazis had bashed the poor wretch to knock him out before burying him alive. Well, for now, Ben would leave him to one of the camp doctors and return when he could.

Later that day, he received a report that the man was conscious and able to speak through an interpreter so paid a visit to Moshe Horwitz, as the patient introduced himself. Qualified watchmaker, he chose to add. Emaciated as he was, he could be any age, although he was unlikely to be over thirty. Somehow or other, he had missed the transportation of Jewish prisoners to Auschwitz but ended up here – almost as bad a fate. Yet, by the merest fluke, he'd survived!

'Lieutenant Benjamin Fletcher of the British Army. You are now my patient – although our doctor will supervise your recovery.'

'Sir, I thank you for my life! I'll be forever in your debt. If I can repay you in any way...'

'Mr Horwitz, that's completely unnecessary. We'll give you all possible medical care to recover from your ordeal, then, along with the other survivors, you'll be driven to the nearby displaced persons camp once it's set up. You've got your life back!'

With a gentle shake of Moshe's hand, Ben left the infirmary. He would have loved to chat more, but duty called. He'd just been briefed – they were taking over a local German Panzer army camp once the surviving prisoners were deloused and could be moved.

On a personal note, Ben wrote himself a reminder to check with the supervising doctor and be there to farewell Moshe when he left. A man snatched from the very jaws of death. That didn't happen every day.

Yes, plenty more jobs to attend to... especially caring for other survivors. Followed by planning the move.

Ben and his fellow officers, turning to the task, did their best to comfort and organise the remaining inmates. They requisitioned basic clothes from the area, and the newly freed prisoners were able to dispose of their filthy uniforms, to be put in piles and burnt. Delousing and treating diseases such as typhus, caught in the filth of the camp, was an absolute priority. As compassionate as they could be, the British did their best with what they had or could commandeer.

One job after another... Eventually, the timetable would be met. Once vacated, the filthy disease-ridden remnant of Bergen-Belsen concentration camp was to be burned to the ground by flame-throwing Bren-gun-carriers to eliminate the typhus epidemic and louse infestation. Not a moment too soon.

During the next two weeks, radio broadcasts kept the occupying British troops in touch with the progress of the war which should surely finish anytime now. Hitler's Nazis were collapsing on all fronts, with the victorious Russians, engaged in a life-or-death struggle in Berlin, sweeping in from the east.

'Good one, chaps!' they greeted each announced step towards final victory.

It would likely all be over by the time the fiery destruction of Bergen-Belsen was completed. German Frisia fell to Canadian and Polish forces. Nazi troops were on the point of surrender in the Netherlands.

'He's topped himself!'

They cheered on hearing of Adolf Hitler's suicide on 30 April. The great dictator was dead at last. He would now face a higher judge.

British forces reached the Baltic at the start of May and halted there by agreement with the Russians. American forces met the advancing Red Army, which had finally conquered Berlin at a great cost to themselves, in Central Germany at Torgau on the Elbe River. With the surrender of all remaining Nazi forces, the war in Europe came to an end on 8 May, to the relief of all.

However, there was no time to relax. The Western Allies, along with the might of the Soviet Union, turned to a fresh task.

That of occupying Germany itself.

CHAPTER TWO

At last, the inevitable celebrations had died down. When Benjamin Fletcher had some time to himself, he thought about how World War Two had changed his life. Mercifully, he had escaped with only one wound requiring hospitalisation, plus a short period of illness, and was very thankful to have survived. What a life he'd had so far.

Ben never knew his father. Second Lieutenant Ezra Fletcher was killed in the Great War on 1 July 1916, the opening day of the Battle of the Somme. Futilely advancing against an entrenched enemy position, his poor father had stopped briefly to give aid to a stricken soldier when he was hit by a burst of machine gun fire. He was killed instantly.

Back home in Cranleigh, a picturesque village about eight miles south-east of Guildford in Surrey, Ezra's widow, Myrtle, took the devastating news with a typical British stiff upper lip even though she was three months pregnant. After all, she was only one of many bereaved that day, with over nineteen thousand men killed on 1 July alone. Hundreds of thousands were to follow in the ongoing battle. It was a bloodbath.

Of course, she continued to grieve – for years – but did so in private.

'Ben,' she urged her only child, 'try to be the man your dear dad would have wanted. God rest his soul.'

For many years, Ezra Fletcher's officer's cap lay on his favourite chair at the dining room table. She dutifully kept it there to be acknowledged at every meal. As a little man, Benjamin would often stand and salute it. Myrtle quietly wept in gratitude at the fine boy her son was becoming.

Myrtle Fletcher scarcely had time to worry about her own future, as she had to provide for Ben and herself. True, she had a meagre war-widow's pension, which helped a little. She decided to open a confectionery shop in Cranleigh's High Street once Ben was old enough to be minded or left in a back room with toys. She was soon known as the 'lolly lady' and became very popular with the local children.

'Sweets for the sweet,' she would say to the many young customers offering their pennies.

After school, young Ben was eager to help and often brought friends keen to try a selection. His popularity only increased as he encouraged his schoolmates to drop by. Fortunately, it wasn't all giveaways, as their mothers also turned up to buy the wares. The only things that suffered were Ben's teeth, which became less than perfect from the sugary treats.

Christianity was an important part of Myrtle's beliefs, and she encouraged Ben along the same path, with her son making many friends at Sunday School. She would collect him at the end of the afternoon class before a treat of 'high tea' in a local café.

Myrtle never remarried or had any prospects of doing so. Thanks to the Great War's carnage, a whole generation of British men was destroyed on the battlefield. There were far too many widows or single women and too few unmarried men still available to woo them. She seemed resigned to her widowhood and busied herself making a living. She received spiritual consolation from her attachment to her local Anglican church, St Nicolas, and in her limited free time, busied herself with social ministries to help disabled war veterans.

Ben loved Cubs, then Boy Scouts, and was as keen as mustard to bellow out his reply to the exhortation each meeting from the group leader to 'Do your best!' Bush walks, camps and practical skills such as knot-tying were right up his alley. He revelled in the exploits of Lord Baden Powell related nightly around the campfire and worked conscientiously for his series of badges. Scouting awoke something deep within the young man.

Then, out of nowhere, an unexpected offer.

'You're so kind, but I can hardly accept your generosity.'

Still, the elderly gentleman, a long-time member of her church congregation at St Nicolas, insisted. He'd pay for Ben to attend the local Cranleigh School as a day boy.

'Don't forget our Parish Council motto, Mrs Fletcher – *Cranleigh Cares*.'

True, she knew its Latin equivalent by heart, so reluctantly agreed.

Despite Ben's prowess with scouting and good marks at school, Myrtle wondered about her only child's future. The Great Depression was in full force when he left school after his senior year. He could have taken on the confectionery business but chose not to. Perhaps he'd had enough of lollies. He took a succession of jobs with no real idea of a career. It was a case of finding whatever work was available.

Still, there were consolations. When he was nineteen, the Regal Cinema opened. 'Let's go to the flicks!' he'd call out to his mates. They were all there on opening night, skylarking around until the usher threatened to eject the lot of them. Going to the Regal became a regular Saturday night activity.

Internationally, the storm clouds began to gather, with the German and Italian dictators on the march. Would his simple life in his village be upset? He wasn't the only one to ask the same question. With each passing year, the news from Europe became grimmer.

Then, when Nazi Germany marched into Austria as the 1930s drew to a close, Hitler eyeing Czechoslovakia as the next target, Ben felt conflict would be inevitable. He was right, analysing the situation with more perceptiveness than many politicians. At a community meeting in the village hall, he stood up and shouted, 'It's coming, you know. We mustn't appease Hitler and Mussolini. Stand up to those bullies! Britain needs to rearm! Now – not a second to lose!'

Not everyone listened. Peace in our time? Would Prime Minister Chamberlain's famous 1938 declaration be justified?

When a second war began in 1939, immediately after the Nazi attack on Poland, Benjamin Fletcher knew what his duty was. He thought of how Lord Baden Powell would have reacted and recalled his idol's spirited and successful defence of Mafeking. He felt it wouldn't be long before Britain faced an even worse and much longer siege. Spurred on by that gloomy thought, he enlisted in the British Army at once. Whatever happened, he'd do his bit.

It was an absolute roller-coaster. Forming part of the British Expeditionary Force sent to France in early 1940, he soon knew what retreat looked like. The German Blitzkrieg hit France like a whirlwind in May of that year, and he and his fellow troops were forced back to Dunkirk for a desperate evacuation. The German Army – the Wehrmacht – had completely outmanoeuvred the British-French coalition. France was about to fall!

'To the boats, you lot!' his officer bellowed. Ordered to scramble aboard a small yacht, he had to even abandon his Lee Enfield .303 rifle. By the time he was placed ashore at Dover, Ben had only the army uniform he was standing up in. He was saved by the skin of his teeth.

'Thank you, Lord!' he uttered. It was amazing that two hundred and thirty thousand British servicemen, along with over one hundred thousand French, had been evacuated. They'd live again.

Yes, an absolute miracle. Saved – but what next?

Following retraining and re-equipping, after fulfilling home-based duties during the Blitz on London and being promoted to sergeant, Ben was posted to North Africa. German general Erwin Rommel was on the attack, sweeping all before him.

There was only one defensive position before Cairo and the likely fall of the Suez Canal: El Alamein.

'Backs to the wall, soldiers! It's do or die!' A new commander, Lieutenant General Sir Bernard Montgomery, assumed command of the Eighth Army. Rommel's last thrust was stopped. Now it was the turn of the British forces.

Rommel was at the end of vastly stretched supply lines and thus vulnerable. Using clever tactics, the British threw the Germans off balance. Through a terrible battle of attrition, their attack thrust into Rommel's Panzer army.

'Get 'em, men!' Ben urged.

They did. Many Nazi soldiers were rounded up at bayonet point. Losses were awful on both sides, but Montgomery's tactics prevailed. The Suez Canal would remain in British hands, an essential supply line safeguarded. Rommel's forces and his fabled Afrika Korps were in retreat.

'Sergeant, time for you to enjoy some home leave!' Ben's officer informed him once that sector was secured. He was certainly grateful. Myrtle Fletcher was delighted to see her strapping son again and hear of his exploits. She never ceased praying for his safe homecoming.

'Ben, I can see the army has become your home,' she reflected. It had given her son a sense of community, with the camaraderie provided by his fellow non-commissioned officers, as well as a sense of purpose, with the war still ongoing. Just a pity about the awful danger. The irony of her late husband's death was he had volunteered for the army, yet as a schoolmaster, he was exempt from military conscription. Ezra Fletcher was a man who felt the call of duty. As did young Ben.

'I guess you're right, Mother. Just as well I've been called back to duty. No more North Africa. Officer training for me here in Blighty and then reassignment.'

So it proved.

Graduating as a first lieutenant, Benjamin had a variety of postings and then, in early 1944, was sent to Salisbury Plain and surrounds in south-western England. Special training. No home leave, and complete security. Beach assault operations were paramount. All hush-hush.

Something very big was on.

- - -

Operation Overlord wasn't merely big – it was huge. The invasion of Normandy to open a second front against Hitler's Germany was meticulously planned, with all ground armies, American and British, under the command of General Montgomery. The Nazis knew it was coming, they just didn't know where. Many in the Wehrmacht expected the assault to be at the narrowest point of the Channel, near Calais. However, the Allies outfoxed them, and even though Erwin Rommel prepared extensive defences on the Normandy beaches, they weren't enough. On 6 June 1944, the massive amphibious assault was launched. Sword and Juno Beaches were allocated to the British.

Landing with his men as part of the Third Infantry Division, Lieutenant Benjamin Fletcher urged them onwards, occupying the eastern end of the beachhead. With shelling from the RAN providing covering power and RAF bomber command doing their best to take out enemy reinforcements, the British surged forward. While not all the objectives for the day were gained, the assault was a success.

'Well done, all ranks! We're on the way!' Ben showered them with well-deserved praise.

Later, with the city of Cherbourg captured, the British turned to their next objective, Caen.

'This won't be easy,' he opined. It wasn't, proving to be a prolonged battle. The city fell only in July. On the last day of the attack, a ricocheting bullet hit Ben's left arm. Suffering a significant wound, he was out of the fighting, evacuated to a hospital in Portsmouth that day on an outbound medical transport.

Ben was to spend several weeks out of action. He appreciated his enforced holiday. The doctors and nurses were concerned about the possibility of infection, and he was one of the first to trial a new miracle drug, penicillin. It worked wonderfully. However, the bullet had damaged some of his tendons, and his lack of mobility was delaying his discharge and return to active duty.

'How are you, old boy?' asked his sudden visitor. 'No need to salute, of course!'

In came his colonel, one Horace Kingsley. Ben sat to attention out of respect. He had heard the colonel was briefly out of the front line visiting wounded Third Infantry Division men.

'On the mend, sir! However, the quacks don't want to send me back yet. The arm tendons are still giving me a bit of gyp.'

'Well, we need you, that's for sure. But not till you can shoot straight. Then you can give the Hun a bit of curry! Fortunately, he's now in retreat. We're moving up the French coast and will be well away from where you copped it.'

'Yes, sir, we're right up on the news with broadcasts all the time.' That they were.

'Look, my young friend, I've been giving some thought to when Fritz runs up the white flag. It'll be a few months off, no doubt, but after that, we could use you for something off-line, I'm sure. Interested?'

'Certainly, sir.'

'Righto. Whitehall has various matters on the boil.' The colonel gestured in the direction of London. 'More on that later. Must go. Toodle-pip!'

'Goodbye, sir. Thanks for your visit.'

Ben knew Colonel Kingsley often had meetings with Military Intelligence, confidential as they were. Officers only.

Intriguing.

CHAPTER THREE

Colonel Kingsley always played his cards close to his chest and quite correctly hadn't disclosed he was booked for a secret flight from London direct to the Pentagon the very next day. There was indeed a certain project on the boil, and he was about to be informed of the details.

Now, with his last and most important hospital visit over, it was a train to London for an overnight stay in the family's comfortable West End flat, followed by examining some Military Intelligence briefing papers.

Colonel Kingsley would need an early night. The next morning, it would be wheels up spot on 0600 for his flight west. Plenty of time then to determine his course of action. What were the Yanks' plans? Fascinating stuff...

'Come right in, Colonel, and take a seat.'

Kingsley's American counterpart, Colonel William Hodges, rose to greet him, as did Hodges's secretary and two other officers. Introductions were brief but friendly.

'Like a coffee? Oh, no, I almost forgot. You Brits prefer tea.'

'Thank you, Colonel. Whatever you have available. Black, no sugar.'

'Well, down to business.' Hodges would waste no time. 'With both our forces now making progress in France, we estimate the European campaign will wrap up in a few months, and we're now planning beyond the Nazi surrender. Both of us have an interest in bringing Japan to its knees, and our present undertaking, the Manhattan Project, aims to do just that. Then we're looking to the post-war situation.'

'Exactly. British Military Intelligence is of the same mind.'

'The USA knows that and is grateful. We're aware this alliance with Stalin will fall apart the moment Hitler's gone. Then we'll be competing with him. Manhattan will develop an atomic bomb – we've been on it for some time – and it's imperative the secret of nuclear fission is kept away from the Soviets. However, Britain, as our major ally, will get to share our secrets, on one condition which I'll get to shortly.'

'Oh, yes?' *Here comes the quid pro quo,* thought Kingsley.

'America, Britain and Russia will certainly occupy Germany once it's defeated. Oh, the French are angling for a small zone, and we can accommodate them too, I suppose. Let's look at the map.'

The British colonel could probably recall all of it by heart but politely glanced over it.

'The Russkis are bound to take a zone in this area.' Hodges pointed. They all agreed. 'There will be numerous German scientists and technicians who've been working on nuclear research for Hitler – unsuccessfully, thank God – who'll want to come over to the West. Most will go to ground and be unable to flee right away. They've also been working on rockets.'

Kingsley winced. Those very V-1 and V-2 rockets were now raining down on London. Almost impossible to intercept.

'So we'll be sending in secret service agents – you're fully aware of our OSS, of course?'

Kingsley nodded. He'd been briefed on the secretive Office of Strategic Services and was keen to know how he could be involved.

'But we need you Brits to do the same. It will be a long campaign over months and years to get them all, since most will be in hiding. They'll have to be winkled out and come over to either of us, bringing their essential papers to increase our atomic program and, more importantly, their rocket research information.'

'Colonel Hodges, Britain will be on board with that. We'll do our bit. We aim to be in the forefront with the latest technology.'

'Great to hear that.' The Americans relaxed. 'May I share why the rocket research is so important? Well, we expect the first atomic weapons to be simply dropped by plane once they're fully developed. However, the USA wants any further delivery – should there be a future war – to be by rocket, propelled from one continent to another. It will be the ultimate weapon. I've devised the name: an Inter-Continental Ballistic Missile or ICBM. We need German expertise to help that project.'

William Hodges was obviously proud of himself. *He could expect a generalship*, the British visitor thought.

'So, getting our hands on all those Germans is paramount. Because Berlin and the surrounding areas, with their research facilities, are certain to be in the coming Russian zone, there are more scientists and technicians there than in the zones your country and ours will occupy. Here's the deal – you help us, and we'll help you. Let's get them out! I doubt they'll need much motivation.'

'Go west, young man?' Kingsley liked his little joke.

'I love your style, Colonel. Agreed? Let's do it.'

Horace Kingsley raised his teacup in salute.

It was game on.

The American OSS and British Military Intelligence were indeed of the same mind.

Urged on by a fanatical Hitler, Nazi Germany had first tried developing nuclear technology during the world war in its quest for powerful weapons. Sadly for Hitler, he worked against his own program by drafting many notable scientists into the Wehrmacht rather than allowing them to work on research.

Over time, the program was split up and essentially fizzled out, although there were many useful research documents and records held by individual scientists. If the Allies were able to collect and unify both the scientists and their documents, it would be very helpful indeed. Left disseminated, those findings were of little use.

Just as vital was the German knowledge on rocket research, given the fearsome threat posed by the 'revenge weapons', the V-1 and V-2 rockets, used for the aerial bombing of British cities in the latter stage of the war, plus some cities in France and Belgium when they were back in Allied hands. Terror weapons. Almost up until the war ended, thousands of civilians were killed and many more wounded.

Both William Hodges and Horace Kingsley were right. Terrible as this was, such knowledge needed to fall into the Western Allies' hands, not the Soviet Union's. An ally of convenience, Stalin wasn't to be trusted. By having the ultimate weapon, the Western powers aimed to prevent the next war, not cause it.

As he flew home eastwards across the vastness of the Atlantic, Horace Kingsley knew exactly what his vital future project would be.

And, more importantly, how it would become a reality.

CHAPTER FOUR

It was October before Ben Fletcher was passed as fit for duty and returned to his unit, by which time the front had moved some way in the direction of Germany. In December, there was the military reverse of the Battle of the Bulge, although the American forces were far more affected than other Allied troops.

The winter of 1944–45 was especially severe, but following Hitler's last-ditch offensive in the west, all the Nazis could do was retreat towards the heart of the Fatherland. The British and American allies were on the march from the west, with the Russians, and other Soviet Union troops, advancing from the east. The Nazis were caught in a gigantic pincer movement. In this way, Ben pressed on with the British forces to where his personal war ceased – the site of the former concentration camp.

If anything, the Nazis preferred to surrender to the Western Allies rather than the Russians. Thus, it was the former who were permitted to sweep ever eastwards, towards the heart of Germany.

Now, in the liberated Bergen-Belsen camp, Benjamin Fletcher shared what he'd learned about the post-war occupation of defeated Germany in a briefing with his subordinates. They were all ears.

'Germany's eastern reaches will be given to Poland by way of compensation – you know, Silesia and East Prussia – although the northern part of the latter will become part of the Soviet Union. Where Königsberg is now. The remainder will have four zones of occupation. A Russian zone in the east, an American zone in the south, a French zone in the south-west and our zone – Britain's – will be in the north. But there's one rub.'

'What's that, sir?'

'Berlin will also be divided into the same four parts. Called sectors.'

'But Berlin is…'

'Exactly. It's right in the Russian zone! According to the agreement, the three Western powers will have right of passage through the Russian zone to Berlin. And the forces of all four nations will have free access around the city.'

'Who decided this, sir?'

'The Yalta Conference earlier this year between Mr Churchill, the late President Roosevelt and the Soviet leader, Josef Stalin.' Yalta, a resort town in the Crimea, had hosted that historic conference, the wintry climate a harbinger of the coming frosty atmosphere between East and West.

'Will it all work?'

The men were becoming toey and somewhat unsettled. Ben picked up on their clear emotion and did what he could to calm their growing concern.

'That remains to be seen. For now, we'll be given the boundary of our zone and the rules of occupation. We could be here for years, although you personally will be free to leave the army once everything's sorted. Hopefully by the end of the year.'

'Thanks for the update, sir.'

Ben breathed a sigh of relief. Whatever the task, they'd get it done.

'You're welcome, men. For now, let's make sure we help the rest of the poor blighters here. They're our immediate priority.'

The British troops were glad spring was well and truly in

evidence, and many of the former prisoners had not only survived but were improving in their physical health, thanks to better rations. The dawn of a new age.

Or was it?

CHAPTER FIVE

'Yes, Prime Minister, I'll be on the first flight to London. Thank you for the invitation.'

Winston Churchill's summons to Colonel Horace Kingsley was just that – hardly an invitation. However, with his leader, diplomacy was always the order of the day. Kingsley had expected the call following his confidential report to Whitehall after last year's urgent mission to the Pentagon.

With the European May Victory Day celebrations just concluded, it was time to get down to business, with the new world order now in effect. There was work to do. Based at what would become the headquarters of the British Occupation Zone in Northern Germany, at Bad Oeynhausen, Kingsley quickly booked a seat on the first available military aircraft.

At fifty years of age, the colonel was every inch a military man. He had served eagerly through the First World War campaigns, starting at Gallipoli, then especially distinguished himself at the Third Battle of Ypres in 1917, where he was both gassed and wounded.

'A shame I never got to charge in on horseback!' he mused while recovering from his wounds. The mud and blood of Flanders had long ago put paid to the tactic of a cavalry charge, something this accomplished horseman deeply regretted. To turn the tide of war, tanks were the order of the day.

'How could such a bizarre innovation be effectively used in battle?' he wondered.

Invalided out of front-line service for the remainder of the war, Kingsley was posted to Brigade, where, as well as employing the new military weapon of armoured tanks, he developed a flair for intelligence work. It was his perceptive analysis of enemy tactics that helped throw into reverse Germany's final attacks on the Western Front in 1918.

He was married to Hermione Featherstonehaugh right after the Armistice, and they loved their life in rural Oxfordshire, especially once they devised their new 'H&H' family crest. Hermione was every bit a match for her handsome husband. An expert breeder of champion thoroughbreds, she was also adept in dressage and showjumping, winning many accolades in local competitions. A great judge of potential equine talent, she put many a steed through its paces.

Three children were born to them, a son and two daughters. Residing in Horace's ancestral home, Kingsley Hall, on the Oxfordshire side of the charming rural village of Charlton, their time as a family was idyllic. Hermione came from the neighbouring hamlet of Newbottle, barely west of Charlton. One would need to go a long way to find a more picturesque setting. Though Horace remained in the military, promoted to the rank of colonel, rural life was as calm as anyone could ask for.

Until a new war erupted like a cataclysm in 1939. Horace was on active service the very day Hitler invaded Poland.

Now, with the war concluded in Europe following years of titanic struggle, Horace Kingsley wondered about Churchill's summons. As his aircraft made its way west to the British capital, he calculated the likely purpose of his trip. No doubt related to his Pentagon report.

A year prior, just as the D-Day preparations were about to swing into effect, Colonel Kingsley had received an invitation to become part of Military Intelligence, hence his mission across the Atlantic to meet Colonel Hodges. With the invasion well underway and the Allied positions consolidated, there was much intelligence to be gathered. In short, what were the Germans up to? How long would they hold out? So, his first assignment was simply to analyse material captured during the invasion and report back to Whitehall. This he did. The Nazis were working frantically to develop massive weapons in a desperate bid to turn the tide of war. Fortunately, the Allied sweep through France was disrupting their plans. All this analysis went back to Whitehall. Some of the V-1 and V-2 rocket sites, which had wreaked such damage on London, were captured, and the threat of aerial bombardment began to lessen.

However, the Nazis had planned far more than V-1 and V-2 rockets. Horace Kingsley suspected those goals might just be on the coming meeting's agenda. He was right.

- - -

'Welcome, Colonel Kingsley. Please come right this way.' The attendant at No. 10 Downing Street was the soul of courtesy and ushered Kingsley along a corridor to the designated meeting room. There, seated, was the prime minister, together with a number of military men, most of whom Kingsley knew. He was gratified when Churchill rose to greet him and shake his hand.

Then it was immediately down to business, led by Churchill.

'First, this is completely confidential.' By now, the door had been firmly closed by the departing attendant. 'For some time, the Americans have been working on the Manhattan Project to develop a fearsome weapon, the likes of which the world has never seen. We are up to speed on this, as Military Intelligence has been fully apprised.'

Churchill nodded in Kingsley's direction.

'We thank God the war in Europe, just concluded, ended before the weapon could be deployed. However, with the battle against Japan still ongoing in the Far East, it could be just the means of bringing that epic struggle to a conclusion.'

There was a collective intake of breath. Only one person present was unsurprised.

'American intelligence, the OSS, has shared with us that, after final testing, the first versions of the atom bomb will be dropped on Japan. Then it will be all over.'

The assembled men practically cheered. One had a tear in his eye.

'Sir, what does this mean for us?' A logical question.

'Gentlemen, this new weapon, not yet finally tested, will be very much in its infancy. Though fearsome in its effect, it will just be the start of a weapons race. Britain must be in the forefront, and it is imperative enemy nations be denied the knowledge to produce it.'

'Hear, hear!'

'Exactly. So the Yanks have cut us a deal.'

'Do tell, Prime Minister!'

'They will share their knowledge with us, allowing Britain to develop its own nuclear weapons program, on this condition: they need more scientific resources, many of which are locked up in Germany. Those scientists who developed Hitler's V-1 and V-2 rockets can be redeployed to help both the American and British programs design more advanced nuclear weapons and the means of their delivery. We've already located some of these people in our new zone of occupation. As have the Americans in theirs.'

Colonel Kingsley spoke. 'Military Intelligence is aware of the challenge, Prime Minister.'

'Correct. It's just this – there are many more eminent scientists hiding in the Russian zone in Eastern Germany. Some in Berlin, others in different towns and cities.'

'We can't trust the Russkis!' one officer interjected.

'Absolutely correct, men. Our alliance with them will soon fall apart, now our common enemy is defeated. In fact, I can see an Iron Curtain descending through Eastern Europe. So it's imperative we spirit those scientists and others useful to our cause out to the West, away from the Russians. I therefore announce the launch of Operation Exit. The mission of Military Intelligence, and our forces in general, is to extract them, as Colonel Kingsley here knows.'

Churchill called on Kingsley to speak.

'Gentlemen, as the prime minister is already aware, we are poised to do exactly that. By mutual agreement, we are about to enter West Berlin as part of the occupying force, even though it is deep within the Russian zone. A strategic coup, if I may say so, a window into Eastern Germany. Western forces, the French, Americans and we British, will also have full military access to the city's Russian sector. That will help.'

'True enough, Colonel.'

'We will use that advantage to good effect and see that our intelligence officers find those Germans useful to our needs. Along with any citizens sympathetic to Western aims. We'll save them from a communist dictatorship.'

Churchill nodded. 'I trust you have someone in mind to lead your mission? I appoint you on the spot to be the commanding officer of our Berlin detachment, the moment we can arrange to go in.'

'Thank you, Prime Minister. Yes, I have a very able officer in mind – a young man with distinguished war service.'

Lieutenant Benjamin Fletcher.

CHAPTER SIX

Once his duty to evacuate the surviving concentration camp inmates was complete, Ben Fletcher was transferred to Bad Oeynhausen in Northern Germany, where there were vast tasks awaiting. Allocating food rations to many starving Germans was a priority, along with rounding up any disaffected Nazi soldiers or even civilian sympathisers. Not to mention being on the lookout for war criminals desperate to elude justice. They had their list.

Pacification was the name of the game. Some of the population were simply grateful the war was over, others were sullen in their resistance. Along with the French and Americans in their zones, the aim was to be firm but fair, in the hope the populace would accept the new reality.

'Hello, Lieutenant. Good to see you again. I trust your wound is healed and the arm is back to full use?' Well, well. Colonel Kingsley had a good memory.

Ben Fletcher stood to attention and saluted.

'Yes, thank you, Colonel. To what do I owe this pleasure?' He knew this wouldn't just be a social call and assumed it was a follow-up to last year's hospital visit.

'You've heard we've just reached agreement with the Russians for our troops to occupy sectors in Berlin?'

Ben nodded.

'I'd like to post you there. There'll be work for you to do. Happy?'

'Certainly, sir.' It would be particularly satisfying to dominate the former enemy capital. To put a final end to the atrocity of Nazism. Ben couldn't wait.

Colonel Kingsley hoped it would be a posting the young lieutenant ultimately thanked him for. Of that, he wasn't sure.

Colonel Kingsley was happy with the location of his sector, with the French above it and the American one below it. Each sector was serviced by its own airport. The French had Tegel, the Americans had Tempelhof and they had Gatow, right on the fringe of their area. Ben Fletcher was to be based not far from the airport.

By agreement, there was both an air and road corridor from the Western zones to reach Berlin, and each of the three Western Allies used both. Military convoys and aircraft were arriving constantly, especially as the occupying Allies set up their different headquarters.

Now it was down to business.

'Lieutenant, first job is to locate certain targeted citizens. Start with those in our sector, then the other two on our side. Later, the more difficult task of some in the Russian sector.' Kingsley gave Ben the list.

They certainly weren't scientists in all probability but useful professional people. Engineers and the like. If they were interested in a life in the West, then the Brits were keen to discuss it. With a knowledge of German, Ben was happy to interview them. Extraction of those in the Western sectors from Berlin was no problem, as they could simply be flown out to the British zone from Gatow. However, any people in the Russian sector would be more of a challenge.

The Russkis wouldn't be happy about those refugees being

spirited away from under their noses. Also, the Western soldiers had to ensure they didn't stray beyond the city limits to the surrounding Russian zone. That was a clear no-no. All part of the essential military briefing.

Kingsley gave Ben a further, highly confidential briefing on his personal mission. He was sworn to secrecy about the coming atom bomb with a wink from the colonel, who was now almost becoming a friend, just as he had been that day he visited Ben in the military hospital in Portsmouth.

'Just tested in New Mexico, old boy. Successfully, I'm told. The Yanks will get ready to drop one soon. Probably two. Horrible, I know, but we've got to finish off Japan. Better than a long, drawn-out campaign. I'd hate to have to invade those islands. Hope they surrender quickly once it's used.'

Ben agreed. It was a terrible weapon, shocking that America had to resort to using it. For his part, he'd keep it out of communist hands at all costs.

Now to the task in hand. Quite a list...

CHAPTER SEVEN

Annabelle Jane Kingsley, the colonel's twenty-two-year-old daughter, would be an asset to any business. Somehow, with the war on, she had managed to acquire an accountancy degree from the London School of Economics, all the while volunteering for different war jobs. Over five years ago, although too young to hold a driver's licence, she had somehow wangled the job of driving an ambulance during the worst of the London Blitz, later nursing wounded soldiers and taking charge of ambulance administration in 1944, during the height of the vicious V-1 and V-2 rocket attacks launched by a desperate Adolf Hitler.

After welcoming a boy, a girl then a second daughter, Annabelle, two years later, the Kingsley family was complete, even though having three children in quick succession had strained Hermione in particular. The colonel loved all his children equally and praised their various achievements. He would often reflect on these in quiet moments with his wife. Roger had served his country creditably during the recent war, and Emma worked in coding at Bletchley Park, vital to the war effort. Then there was Annabelle…

'She's right out of the top drawer, that one!' he often confided to Hermione. They all were.

Now, with peace, once she had completed her ambulance administration work by the spring of 1946, Annabelle was keen to put her accounting skills to good use. Where better than in the British sector of occupied Berlin, under her father's watchful eye?

Horace Kingsley was well-served with his eagle-eyed daughter, her work complemented by his keen secretary, Jennifer Rownton, who was married to one of the NCOs attached to Berlin headquarters. Each day, Jennifer would bring in the day's dispatches and orders, dutifully placing them on Colonel Kingsley's desk. Annabelle would busy herself with analysis of the unit's financial details, carefully preparing profit and loss sheets and the like. Jennifer and Annabelle were a formidable team.

Many a soldier noted that while Jennifer was happily married to a man satisfied with life in the service, Annabelle was single and a free spirit. Possibly not destined to always be part of a military unit. Although a valuable member of one for now.

'Delighted to meet you, Miss Kingsley. I'm Lieutenant Benjamin Fletcher.' She knew that already but was impressed by his polite introduction. Annabelle was extremely astute and fully aware of new appointees and their backgrounds, having diplomatically asked her father for details, all the while appearing as carefree about the information as possible.

He continued, 'Can you please tell me what you're working on? I'm in the Civilian Liaison Unit and responsible for...' It hardly had anything to do with accounting, but she was happy to share her work interests with this handsome young officer.

Jennifer gave Annabelle a subtle wink. 'Can I bring you both a cup of coffee? I guess you've got plenty to discuss.' Then, she discreetly withdrew.

Over time, Ben looked for more and more opportunities to share events with the attractive Miss Kingsley. By the next year, a budding romance blossomed, despite Ben being often away from headquarters interviewing likely refugees throughout Berlin. He was always ready to spring into action at a moment's notice.

'Lieutenant, an urgent message from Pankow District.' An alert from a duty officer manning the British Army headquarters hotline for would-be refugees, the number discreetly disclosed on the East Berlin grapevine. Ben was on call.

He was soon away, accessing the city centre and then heading north, his entry to that sector noted by the Russian border guards. Arriving at the grimy house, part of which had been damaged extensively by Allied bombing, he was greeted with a firm handshake from an eager man.

'Pleased to meet you, sir. I am Jens Becker.'

The two of them made sure the door was closed immediately to avoid any report from the patrolling Russians. Or, even worse, one of their Ministry of State Security agents. Ben was introduced to the man's wife and two small daughters.

'Sir, can you get our family out to the West? I have detailed engineering material valuable to the Western Allies. I don't want it to fall into Russian hands.'

Ben quickly perused the file. Though not a scientist himself, he could tell it was clearly valuable. He set a plan in motion.

'Tomorrow, Frau Becker, put your basic requirements into a small suitcase, take your girls and cross into the French sector at the Pankow border point. From there, you will find transport to Grünewald in our area. If quizzed, say you are going shopping in West Berlin. Thank heavens the Russians are still permitting this.'

'Thank you!'

'And you, Herr Becker, will put your essentials in a work briefcase, for a "business meeting" in the American sector. From which point you will rendezvous at Grünewald with Frau Becker and the girls. At the refugee centre, you will be provided with rather more than the bare essentials you'll be able to bring with you.'

'And do you fly us out to your British zone?'

'Exactly. There will be a new life for you in the West. Just make sure you bring your "business meeting" file with you.'

'I will. Goodbye, Lieutenant, and thank you.'

'You're welcome. Goodbye for now.'

Driving back to base through Pankow, the young officer failed to note a passer-by recording his British numberplate. Captain Sergei Chekhev of the Soviet Ministry of State Security, the MGB, had seen the same vehicle a number of times in his sector. While it was officially permitted, it was still suspicious. What was the Britisher doing?

Analysing the pattern of visits, which corresponded to numerous citizens in the visited areas vanishing to the West, led Chekhev to the inescapable conclusion. He was helping people get out! That, Chekhev must stop.

Back in his headquarters close to the city centre, the MGB agent got out his file. There were the photos of three military cars the Britisher had used, with a fleeting one of the man himself. Blast his luck – the photo was far from clear. Then, here was the record of the missing citizens. Interesting – all were qualified Germans, useful in some way to any society.

So where had that man visited in Pankow? Perhaps local officers in the occupying Red Army might know. Time for a check.

– – –

It was a blessing indeed Russian military intelligence was less effective than usual that day. By the time Chekhev's enquiries had narrowed Ben Fletcher's visit location down to a certain house in Morgenstrasse, and the alert was put out to crossing points the next morning, Frau Becker and her two daughters had just passed through their designated one and were vanishing into a crowd in the French sector.

'Where's her damned husband?' Chekhev bellowed in frustration. 'He must have gone somewhere else. Repeat the alert!'

They did.

Jens Becker was entering the Neukölln crossing point when the phone rang. The Russian on duty had just lit up a Gauloises cigarette he'd won from a French soldier he was chummy with. Beat him at cards! No, he wanted a deep puff before answering.

By the time he did so, the German fugitive was safely in the American sector.

'Sorry, Commander. We've just missed him!'

Who cared? Just another German, and it was time for a smoke.

Frustrated by his failure, Captain Chekhev put in an official complaint to the British, this coming through to Colonel Kingsley.

'Ben.' Kingsley accosted him the moment he read it. 'Berlin's getting too hot for you. I've got an even more important assignment for you...' Ben had been in the former capital since mid-1945, and it was now well into 1947.

'Yes, Colonel?'

'Plenty to do elsewhere. Undercover in the Russian zone. There'll be training here over winter, then a transfer west to our zone for follow-up work before your field assignments.'

Ben whistled. He wasn't expecting that. Just before his first training course, he had an important matter to attend to. He proposed marriage to Annabelle, and she accepted, smothering him in kisses.

He'd be very careful with each assignment. He had a lot to live for.

CHAPTER EIGHT

In late winter 1948, his Berlin training complete, Ben took a military transport to Bad Oeynhausen in the British zone for advanced German language study. While he was already competent in the language thanks to intensive work in the former capital, the Saxon dialect of the Russian zone had its challenges, and he had to be fluent. As well, he had to be knowledgeable about local geography, even down to a small-town and village level. The geography teacher took him through the major cities and towns for a start.

'Apart from Berlin, which you know well, others are Magdeburg, Halle, Leipzig, Dresden and Karl-Marx-Stadt. Their industries are as follows...' All this information was dutifully recorded in his notebook, for committing to memory.

'Please explain the small towns. I'll need to know about them.'

'Certainly. You'll be working in Thuringia, where you'll find Erfurt, Weimar and Jena. Further afield, I may need to mention Zwickau, south-west of Karl-Marx-Stadt. Now, from a historical point of view, Weimar was known for...' More facts for the notebook.

Soon, Ben was competent in all the regions of the zone, as far east as the new Polish border. Would his mission take him as far as Cottbus or Frankfurt on the Oder?

'Lieutenant Fletcher, I'm British Command's political officer, Major Cummins!'

'Sir!' He sat to attention. Major Cummins was in charge of assessing military developments affecting the British zone and advising on the likely threat level posed by the Red Army occupying their zone of Germany. Political changes were exactly his specialty. He'd been with the military throughout the entire war, spoke Russian and was in the forefront of the British defence effort.

'At ease, Lieutenant. I'll now take you through developments in the Russian zone since the Soviets began their occupation. Some of this material is quite confidential for now. Briefly, the Russians are about to start forming their zone into a client state, although we estimate it won't be announced until sometime next year. Nevertheless, the transformation is well underway. You're familiar with the term Iron Curtain, first used by Churchill over a year ago?'

'Certainly, sir.'

'Well, it's very apt. We have just such a curtain separating the Western nations from the communist powers. Let's look at the details...'

Ben had to acknowledge the Red Army, which had swept through eastern Europe in 1945, had thrown up many communist regimes in its wake. A real challenge for the West.

Then to the confidential briefing about what Major Cummins called the coming German Democratic Republic. It would be politically separate from the three Western zones, which were to amalgamate into the Federal Republic of Germany. Cummins stressed this would definitely happen. Already, there was barbed wire dividing the Russian zone from the others.

'It'll get worse. There'll be a whole network to deter escapees. They'll still come, mark my words. Over time, communism can't compete with freedom in the West.'

Cummins had certainly done his research.

Ben studied the major's projections for what would be called East Germany. Communist doctrine laid it all out neatly. He had much to study and absorb, all of it very important.

Then he looked at the next item on his training schedule. A practical one: hand-to-hand combat and judo instruction, something he had undertaken once in officer training, but he needed a refresher.

The lieutenant was prepared to come to grips with any situation, one might say.

CHAPTER NINE

In 1935, Reinhard Schwarz knew it was time to go. The twenty-four-year-old had heard through the grapevine the Gestapo were on the lookout for him. Dedicated to Communist Party goals since his youth, once arrested, his sure destination would be a concentration camp, from which he might never emerge. Communists were one of dictator Adolf Hitler's pet hates, and he showed them no mercy.

Reinhard was the eldest of four children. His two younger brothers had not the slightest interest in his political leanings, and he felt little in common with them, often arguing against their clear apathy. Only his sister, Helga, born much later in 1925, was of a similar disposition to him. In fact, Helga almost worshipped her oldest brother and lapped up what he and their father spouted. Reinhard, flattered, did everything he could to encourage her.

'OK, Helga – here are the words of the *Internationale*. Let's sing. One, two, three...!'

Even as a young girl, she was fully indoctrinated. He, in turn, was greatly influenced by their father Manfred's constant utterances and propaganda speeches. With Frau Schwarz trying to appease everyone to maintain domestic peace, it was an interesting household.

'Live for Bolshevism, Reinhard!' His son heard this catchcry from his war veteran father many times, recalling it especially often since the poor man's death two years previously. Manfred Schwarz lived for that movement and had done so since hearing about the glorious Russian Revolution while he recovered from his wartime maiming.

Eager to serve the Kaiser in the Great War, Manfred Schwarz had volunteered for the German army the moment hostilities were declared in 1914. Held in reserve initially, he was thrust into the massive 1916 onslaught against Verdun. The French resistance was fanatical, and after a month of vicious fighting, an enemy artillery shell took off his lower right leg. The pain and shock were indescribable.

The field doctor had many more wounded to attend to, and the amputation had to be done with copious doses of whisky as an anaesthetic and a little medication. Manfred barely survived.

Invalided home, the disabled veteran was an easy mark for revolution. The whole family, especially young Reinhard, had suddenly fallen out of love with the Kaiser, all the more so as the prospects of winning the war dimmed and then vanished altogether. The emperor's abdication in November 1918 failed to meet their perceived need of justice. The events in Russia impressed them more.

'That's what we want, revolution in Germany! Bring it on! Get rid of every imperialist. We need socialism!'

It became a family mantra, at least between the father and his eldest son.

Post-war inflation destroyed what savings the family had, and they were practically destitute. The Weimar Republic, encouraged by the victorious Allies, did little to meet their needs. Germany was a basket case.

Bitter and depressed, Manfred took to drink, dying from alcoholic poisoning in 1933, the month after Hitler came to power.

Reinhard was made of sterner stuff and pledged to work his fingers to the bone to bring in Bolshevism, whatever it took.

Stalin's methods in Russia suited him just fine. Politically, he hated Hitler's terror from the Right. Stalin's terror from the Left troubled him not a bit. On his bedroom wall, he hung the banner *'The end justifies the means!'* He meant every word of it.

However, for now, he needed to make himself scarce. Time to go. Down came the banner and into a suitcase. He was sorry he'd have to leave little Helga behind, but she'd be alright. It couldn't be helped.

A native of Zwickau, a town just above the Czech border, Reinhard quickly packed the rest of what he needed into the same suitcase, leaving his home without any farewells. Then he secretly made his way into Czechoslovakia through a forested area. Having acquired a stash of money courtesy of Party officials, and armed with his passport, he caught a bus to Prague, from where he bought a plane ticket to Moscow, a circuitous flight through Warsaw.

With his carefully prepared credentials, Reinhard was warmly welcomed by Party officials there. After some orientation, it was decided he was fit for appropriate work in Leningrad – the former St Petersburg, Russia's window on the Baltic. Mastering Russian was no great effort, and within a year, Reinhard was happily ensconced in his new location. Much of his task was to prepare to eventually re-enter Germany once the conditions were favourable. Which would be some time off.

'How could Comrade Stalin do that?' he screamed in frustration to his girlfriend, Lena, one day in August 1939. 'Sign a non-aggression pact with Hitler? What was he thinking?' It was an uncharacteristic outburst.

All was revealed in September when the Nazis attacked Poland, quickly occupying the western half. The Red Army moved into the east of the conquered country under the terms of a secret protocol in the pact. A devious act by both dictators. Politically, Poland was no more.

'It's war, Lena – war!' Reinhard yelled once more at the news the Nazis had double-crossed the Soviet Union by attacking on a wide front in June 1941. The Great Patriotic War involving Mother Russia fighting for her very existence had begun. He and Lena were married, and she was expecting her first child any day now.

Volunteering for the Red Army, Reinhard Schwarz joined Leningrad's elite battalion to move west and engage the Nazis. However, so dramatic was Hitler's blitzkrieg that they were quickly forced back to defend the besieged metropolis. It was to the battlements indeed.

'We're starving, Reinhard! Can you get some food for the baby?' was his poor wife's desperate plea. He scavenged whatever food he could.

As the months passed into a year or more, starvation was as dangerous as the relentless Nazi shelling. There were no longer any stray dogs to be found anywhere. They had gone to dinner tables ages ago. Famine stalked the streets.

The only consolations for Reinhard were his military duties often intersected with times of home leave, given the front line was where the civilians were, and Red Army rations were a little better than the meagre allocation given to non-combatants. Eventually, there was nothing at all for them. In utter desperation, they'd eat grass and weeds, all in the shadow of the grim reaper.

'Lena,' he called as he approached his bombed-out house while on brief leave from the front line, 'I've found a crust of mouldy bread. Enough for a couple of bites. One for you, and the baby can suck on the other.'

It was too late. The home was now silent. He found them both emaciated and lifeless, starved to death. They were just two more to add to the growing pile of corpses.

Ironically, the siege was lifted two months later, with the Nazis unable to take the city. Leningrad was saved. Throwing himself afresh into the war effort, Reinhard moved west with his battalion to engage the slowly retreating Nazi hordes, who were demoralised by their military failure and exhausted by the vast extent of Russia.

The campaign for liberation was slow but relentless. Fighting in western Russia, then Poland, demolished the Nazi positions as the Reds moved ever westwards. East Prussia was gone. Then the titanic battle for Berlin caused huge losses for both sides. With the much-despised capitalist forces, Stalin's derisively named 'little Allies', sweeping across Germany from the west, the Nazis finally surrendered on 8 May.

The war in Europe was all over.

Reinhard had no reason to return to Russia. His aim would now be achieved. Socialism in the very heart of Germany, courtesy of the occupying Red Army – they would guarantee that. A political commissar with his battalion, he knew what the future would be and was determined to be part of it. He let his superiors know he would take on any task to help organise the present zone into a unified state the Kremlin would be proud of. 'Please inform Comrade Stalin!'

They did. Reinhard was tasked with getting to work immediately. A four-year program was outlined.

When that was done by the target year of 1949, with hoped-for personal glory, he would have only one more step to take. By hook or by crook, he'd create the opportunity. Extend socialism to the west.

He could then rest easy in his earthly paradise.

CHAPTER TEN

'Great – five flashes!' They were coming, having answered his three flashes of the torch. The agreed signal.

On this moonless night at the safest crossing point due east of the base at Bad Oeynhausen, Ben Fletcher watched for them scrambling under the barbed wire. There they were, five figures.

He desperately hoped it wasn't a trap, with the would-be refugees then cut down by a hail of Russian gunfire. No, they were fine, running across the open ground, safely into the British zone.

Crouched in a group of small trees, Ben flashed his torch once more, and they were excitedly greeting him. '*Danke Gott. Wir sind frei!*' Yes, praise God indeed for your freedom. Seconded to Military Intelligence, Ben was happy to help.

Over several weeks, there were similar escapes by Germans keen to resist their Russian occupiers and yearning for what the West offered. The Allied forces especially encouraged those with useful skills. A knowledge of nuclear technology put them at the top of the list. Many a briefcase full of research papers went either to the Americans or the desk of British Military Intelligence, its preferred destination.

Ben was getting used to his period of 'reception duty' when he was ordered to ratchet his efforts up a notch. His next mission would be 'over the border'. But first, some essential preparation. As Colonel Kingsley put it in his phone call, 'Old boy, you're destined for great heights!'

Thus, a refresher course in parachute jumping under the tutelage of the best specialist in the forces, one Jock MacTavish. Two weeks' intensive training.

'I reckon you're guid to go, laddie!' exclaimed the cheery Scotsman after a final parachute jump, completed with precision in open countryside just out of Bad Oeynhausen. Jock really liked his 'wee Sassenach', as he fondly called his student. Ben, at five feet nine inches, was no midget but paled into insignificance beside his instructor, who towered over him at six feet eight.

Getting his training award that spring day, Ben shook hands with Jock, who gave him a celebratory hug. 'Guid luck with it all' was his fond farewell. Not all his graduates survived field conditions. Some had been known to vanish without trace. All Jock could do was ensure they were well-trained. That he did without fail.

Then, for Ben, it was down to a mission briefing – he would be extracting a small group from Weimar, right in the 'bulge' of the Russian zone. Ben scrutinised his notes. Weimar was a university town once associated with the famous German writer Johann Wolfgang von Goethe. In the present day, it featured considerable tertiary research. A small group of scientists had amassed material useful to the developing British nuclear program. Eager to come over to the West, neither those professionals nor the Allies wanted it to fall into Russian hands.

His superior officer made the instruction clear.

'Lieutenant, the Russkis are nosing around Weimar, realising something's up. It's only a matter of time before they put enough troops on the ground to sweep through the town and round up the Germans. Then that research will be lost. Get there before they do!'

No room for doubt. Fortunately, they had one advantage. Weimar was not too far from the zone border. Once across, they'd be safe. He'd give it a go. Travelling by night through the last stretch, the goal was reachable.

'Zero hour is 2100. Be packed and ready.'

With his kit well-prepared, he was.

The RAF bomber departed the runway right on 2100 hours with a flawless take-off in the hands of its skilled pilot, who set his course eastwards. Ben noticed extra tension both in himself and his teammates as they neared the border. Would the Soviets tumble to what they were doing? What if they dispatched one of their Yakovlev Yak-3s? Would the RAF bomber elude it, or would the Russians open fire?

His fears were groundless, as the co-pilot called out, 'Five minutes to go. Final parachute check!'

Ben did exactly that and consulted his watch. They were right on time. As the plane door opened, there was a final shout of 'Good luck!' and Ben was airborne.

Tumbling earthwards through the calm night, he activated his chute, which was surprisingly easy to control in the benign conditions. The pilot had done his job well, and Ben was as close to the designated drop zone as was possible. Landing was coming up, right in the middle of a clear field. He braced for impact.

Jock's training had served him well, and he hit the ground running, gratefully collapsing into his parachute. He was safely down. Gathering up his fallen chute, he made for the cover of a nearby forest, where he concealed its remains in some bushes, using the trenching tool in his pack to add to the effort.

According to his calculations, Weimar was no more than two miles away, and he set off, careful to only walk along the path when it was deserted. His compass confirmed the direction. His estimate was spot on – there he was in town. No evidence of any patrolling Russians. Thank heavens they couldn't be everywhere.

Now to Number 25 Hofgasse and his meeting. The house had only one light on, and he gently knocked, calling out '*Morgenlicht*.' From inside came the prearranged reply, '*Abendlicht*.' Noting the door was unlocked, Ben Fletcher entered.

'Guten Abend, Doktor Trumm. Wie geht's?'

With the niceties over with after much handshaking and the offer of schnapps from the good doctor, they turned to the business at hand. Doktor Trumm was alone for now, but three colleagues would join them in the morning, and all four of them, plus Ben, would take the town bus as far westwards as was allowed. Should any police – or, heaven help, Russian soldiers – indicate interest, they would show their papers stating a scientific excursion was the order of the day. Ben's false papers were the same. Once night fell, they would cross the border under that cover.

'Herr Fletcher, I thank you for discovering the exact weak point in the border crossing and being prepared to guide us over. Better than the hit-or-miss method of trying to work it out for ourselves.' British Military Intelligence had been hard at work.

'You're welcome, Herr Doktor!'

The academic was a spritely man in his mid-fifties, trimmer than many of his age. He had a receding hairline and wore glasses. Immaculately dressed in a three-piece suit, he looked as though he was about to give a university lecture, as he had no doubt done many times. Trumm eagerly quizzed Ben about security at the border and made a mental note of his reply. The lieutenant was happy to elaborate.

Those weak points changed frequently, depending on the means available to the patrolling Russians at any given time. Hence the need for a guide. Following Ben's explanation, with a bed provided, he turned in for a restless sleep.

Punctually at 8 a.m. the next morning, the three companions arrived. After hurried introductions, the five of them set off. The town bus departed at 8.30. In two groups, they boarded. This one would take them as far as Gotha, with a final journey closer to the border.

Doing their best not to attract attention, they travelled on, appearing as nonchalant as possible. To look the part, they occasionally produced harmless scientific papers relating to the environment and shared some comments. None of the other passengers showed much interest.

Traversing Erfurt, the next stop was Gotha, where they alighted. With a wait of thirty minutes until the final bus leg, they adjourned to a coffee shop. Unfortunately, two police officers were patrolling and noticed the strangers.

'Papers, please!'

The group promptly obeyed. Scrutinising them, the police seemed satisfied. 'Scientific excursion, is it? I hope you make some good discoveries!'

Everyone laughed. For the group, simply in relief. They froze again when a Russian military patrol drove by, although it kept going. Tension relaxed.

The bus was five minutes late departing. All exhaled in gratitude when it finally did. Gotha could have been a close one.

Just on dusk, there ahead was their terminus at Bad Salzungen, and somewhat weary from the stress, the two groups stepped off. Now to the final stretch on foot, just as dusk was falling.

Using a waterproof map, Ben guided the fugitive academics, who clutched their briefcases of precious scientific papers. As the hours passed and they walked in the dark without complaint through an increasingly forested area, he calculated that the present minimally patrolled section was no more than a mile ahead.

Ideally, it would be better to time their escape for just on dawn, with a little light to help. However, the danger of hanging around in the forest for hours outweighed the dawn advantage. They needed to make their break now.

'*Meine Herren*, not far to go now!'

Their resolve stiffened, but so did the tension. Then, there it was. Barbed wire. Ben ordered complete silence and instructed them to group about forty yards from the wire in whatever cover was available. Going forward alone, from his pack he took out four props, each attached to a length of thin rope.

'Carefully does it...' went his self-talk as he inserted each prop under a section of wire, lifting it. If they crawled low enough, the good doctors could just get to the other side without injury.

Rejoining the group, he urged them forward. 'Get down low and go, go, go!' he whispered. 'Then regroup in those trees over there when you get through. I'll follow.'

They needed no further urging, quietly wriggling under the vicious wire with a fitness and skill that belied their advancing years. They were through!

Ben followed and, on finding refuge on the other side, just before likewise sprinting over to the designated trees, pulled on the ropes and retrieved the props, which went back into his pack.

'Leave no evidence! No point in giving the Russkis a free kick!'

Otherwise, he urged silence until they were out of range of parting shots from the Russians, should any come. None did.

Then they whooped and hollered like men possessed, the tension broken. Their university students would have shaken their heads in dismay at seeing their profs now.

'OK, let's walk in the direction of Bad Hersfeld and hope we stumble upon a farmhouse before we get too footsore.' Some of them had blisters by now but hardly noticed.

Minutes later, there was their salvation, a farmhouse. Banging on the surprised farmer's door, they were welcomed inside with hearty congratulations from the good man and his wife, who were ready to turn in for the night.

They realised not every escape bid was successful. Others would be shot to death, tangled in the barbed wire. This one was a cause for celebration.

The group was given emergency bedding but could hardly sleep for excitement. They were free! At dawn, the happy farmer phoned the American forces, and a truck duly arrived to transport them to the nearest base. There, Ben reported to the commander, who offered his hearty congratulations and transport for all north to the British zone.

As the young agent bade farewell to the refugees, with their precious nuclear information destined for Britain, one gratefully asked, 'What next for you, Herr Fletcher?'

He was stunned to hear the quick reply.

'Me? Oh, I'm getting married in a week. Quite an adventure!'

Perhaps the good prof thought it held just as many dangers as being a secret agent.

CHAPTER ELEVEN

The Church of St Giles south of Kingsley Hall in rural Oxfordshire was resplendent with decoration the June day blushing bride Annabelle Jane Kingsley entered its doorway, joyfully on the arm of her father, Horace. There at the side of the altar stood her soon-to-be husband, Benjamin, flanked by his best man and groomsman, both friends in the service.

In the front row, next to Hermione Kingsley, sat Ben's proud mother, Myrtle. Even before the engagement, the two mothers had become great friends, and Myrtle Fletcher was often a guest at Kingsley Hall, which was no more than two miles from St Giles. Neither woman could suppress a happy tear at the coming union as they clutched each other's arms.

Annabelle's best friend, Jennifer Rownton, was her matron-of-honour, and her older sister, Emma, a bridesmaid. On the other side of the altar stood St Giles's rector, Rev. Archibald Thompson. He positively beamed with pleasure, happy to perform another service for the Kingsley family. Post-wartime restrictions, which included continual rationing, were the only impediment to an otherwise delightful ceremony and the coming festivities.

'Love is patient and kind. Love is not jealous or boastful… it does not demand its own way. It rejoices whenever the truth wins out. Love never gives up.'

Hearing Rev. Thompson preach that well-known but

appropriate message from the Book of Corinthians, Ben Fletcher resolved never to give up.

'Three things will last forever – faith, hope and love – and the greatest of these is love.'

Indeed it is and always will be.

As Ben exited the church with his new bride on his arm, they received the usual military salute under an archway of crossed swords. An absolute delight. Following the reception in the adjacent church hall, albeit one still subject to food rationing, the happy couple were soon on their way by train to their honeymoon location, a hotel on the south coast at Brighton. There, the troubles of post-war Germany were to be put to one side for the next fortnight while the newlyweds got to know each other.

Blessed also by pleasant, sunny weather – not always a given – they were contemplating the final two days of their stay when there was a knock on their hotel room door. Puzzled, Ben opened it. There stood the manager.

'Lieutenant Benjamin Fletcher? A telegram.'

He took it. They could have done without this.

'*Return to base in Bad O. immediately. Stop. Russians blockade Berlin. Stop. Emergency action. Message ends.*'

It was a day the couple would never forget – 24 June 1948, the start of the infamous Berlin Blockade.

Trust Josef Stalin to spoil the end of a honeymoon.

CHAPTER TWELVE

'Ben, old boy, your new assignment. From zone headquarters, keep our garrison here in Berlin and the whole sector supplied. The Russkis won't break us. We'll cut rations to the bone if necessary.'

'Will do, sir! I'm right onto it...'

Colonel Kingsley had been insistent, hardly waiting for Ben's plane to land before phoning. Patience was hardly one of the man's virtues.

The newlywed lieutenant wondered if his corpulent father-in-law would now start a diet. No bad thing and a definite advantage once he had the chance to get back to some horseriding.

Now back in Bad Oeynhausen and quickly ensconced in married quarters there, Ben got right to work. Breaking the blockade by a massive airlift, in conjunction with the United States Air Force, was an absolute priority. Stalin, dirty over several issues brought in by the Allies, including the introduction of the new currency to Berlin, the Deutsche Mark, had imposed a blockade which covered railway, road and canal access to the three Western sectors. The city was isolated.

You could just hear him exulting in the Kremlin. 'Comrades, we'll starve them out! They'll slink off with their tails between their legs!' An undisclosed reason for the blockade was the leaking of citizens from his zone – those miserable worms and traitors doing their best to escape communism. Yes, he'd had reports of Allied ringleaders conspiring to entice otherwise-loyal subjects away from the workers' paradise of the Soviet zone, and that he'd put a stop to. For now, he'd starve his former 'little Allies' out of West Berlin, then he'd choke off the escapee flow. Now, where was his special file?

The Allies were determined to survive and brought in a massive airlift to ensure the city was kept supplied. British, American and French headquarters were buzzing with frantic activity. Soon, a fleet of Douglas C-54 Skymasters and C-47s, great transport planes, were pressed into service. Food and fuel were priorities, with thousands of tons to be delivered daily. The Allies rose to the challenge magnificently. The citizens loved it.

Initially, as part of the British team, Ben was working around the clock to set the system in motion. The Hamburg and Buckeburg air corridors, the only ones permitted by the Russians, were filled constantly with aircraft flying to Berlin, unloading at Gatow Airport, then returning for more supplies. The French joined them, employing Tegel Airport to good effect. The Americans used their Frankfurt corridor efficiently, landing at Tempelhof. Russian fighters often buzzed the planes aggressively, but mercifully didn't open fire.

Air crews from Commonwealth countries – Canada, Australia, New Zealand and South Africa – joined the RAF, and Ben had an important liaison role with them. He got on famously with all of them.

Lording it over his underlings in the Kremlin, an increasingly frustrated Stalin considered launching all-out military action to achieve what the blockade was failing to accomplish but hesitated for one reason. 'The cursed Americans have the atom bomb, and we don't!' At least, not yet.

He'd redouble his efforts in that direction. For now, the ruthless dictator was bruised, defeated by Allied efficiency and sheer will. There was no way they'd abandon West Berlin, or the

German people. Stalin had to seek consolation where he could. Time for a rethink.

The traffic to the three airports was constant. At the height of the airlift, one plane reached West Berlin every thirty seconds. The besieged city survived the bitter winter, despite the frigid conditions, and as spring set in, there was hope. Would the Russians back down?

They did.

'We've done it, Annie!'

An ecstatic Ben whirled his wife around and then, thinking better of it, gently brought her back to earth. 'Sorry, for a moment I forgot you were pregnant.' She certainly was, and due in four months. Equally delighted, however, Annabelle Fletcher didn't mind a bit – 12 May 1949 was a happy day for all concerned. Just like V-E Day four years before.

'Yep, Stalin's backed off and the roads are open again. Dad in West Berlin will be happy for his troops. They'll be off their iron rations.'

'And he'll be back on his favourite port after dinner.' Such was the effect of the imposed restrictions.

'Like everyone there, he's been through a real storm. Had to scrounge whatever port he could find.'

Ben couldn't resist a smile for his dear wife.

'Well, as they say, any port in a storm!'

Touché.

CHAPTER THIRTEEN

'Get me General Volsky on the phone – now!' Stalin almost barked at his hapless secretary. The Soviet leader was in a paranoid fury the week after he'd been forced to call off the Berlin blockade, unable to work out how the much-maligned West had outfoxed him. Practically locked in his office, reeking from constant cigar smoke, his rubbish bin overflowing with empty vodka bottles, he wasn't to be trifled with. She did as ordered.

His mood with his contact general in Germany wasn't much better. 'So, tell me again who that political commissar working on our new state for East Germany is?'

'Reinhard Schwarz, Comrade Stalin.'

Volsky thought it better not to remind the dictator the name was clearly in the German file and had been for four years. A wise move. When in such a foul mood, Stalin was in the habit of sending out the latest list of imagined enemies to face a firing squad. Volsky hoped never to be on it.

Now remembering the name as his hangover began to lift, Stalin went on. 'He must have almost finished his organisation by now. I know the target date is coming up.'

'Yes, indeed, Comrade Stalin. He has only the finishing touches to complete.'

'Good. I have a new assignment. Here are the details…'

General Volsky made sure to have his secretary listen in to the call, keen to ensure he missed nothing. She took frantic shorthand notes. Yes, deal with that other running sore – escapees to the West – get Schwarz right onto it – infiltrate any known escapee organisations and stop them – shoot on sight at the border but keep within the damn rules. Then seal the frontier to keep the fascists out.

Stalin was also furious the three Allies, as well as unifying their zones into the Federal Republic of Germany any day now, had last month formed a defence pact, the Northern Atlantic Treaty Organisation – NATO. His only consolation was the Soviets now had the means, largely acquired from spies, to detonate their first atomic bomb, with the first nuclear test scheduled for late August. There would be more, of that he was determined.

'Thank you, Comrade Stalin. I'll get Schwarz right onto it.'

'Make sure you do.' Slightly mollified, the dictator hung up. Then opened another bottle to celebrate...

Reinhard Schwarz had certainly been very industrious in his determination to bring about the formation of an approved socialist state in the very heart of Germany, greatly helped by many in the occupying Russian army. Taking the well-known motto *'Workers of the World, Unite!'* he had proposed the new official name for East Germany and delegated a team of musicians to compose its anthem, *Risen from Ruins*. Both he and the Kremlin were delighted with the result. Stirring indeed. The German Democratic Republic would be a world leader of the socialist struggle.

Yet the Soviets ensured the GDR would remain their satellite state. All the above was mere window-dressing. The proof was that their forces were destined to remain there indefinitely – of course, to deter NATO aggression. Secretly, the army was to prepare a contingency plan to launch an assault on Western

Europe, should political opportunities align. In any case, the Red Army was to be battle-ready.

With the target date of 7 October 1949 locked in for the announcement of the new state, and German communist leaders having taken over administrative responsibility the year before, Reinhard Schwarz was ready to work on his plan to tighten up every possible law to eliminate dissent. Establishing a security service was a priority.

When General Volsky summoned him to headquarters, his new task was right in line with his thinking. OK, another immediate job. A little later, the security service. For now, stop the leakage of escapees. He went over to his firearm cabinet, which held every weapon he was likely to need, and made his selection.

Death to would-be refugees.

'Well, sir, to what do I owe this pleasure?' Ben Fletcher was slightly surprised by Colonel Kingsley's unannounced visit to headquarters in Bad Oeynhausen in September.

He soon found out.

'My boy, I'm reluctant to trouble you with this, but I'm afraid it's urgent. Particularly as things are – er – delicate with Annabelle at the moment.' This was his very English way of acknowledging his daughter was due to give birth within a fortnight.

He didn't beat about the bush. Just to the east of the British zone, which was now part of the Federal Republic of Germany, a final group of three physicists was seeking refuge in the West. As before, they held vital information for the developing British nuclear weapons program. They'd fled their homes, and the Russians were on their tail. Far better to secure them and their expertise working for Military Intelligence than for Josef Stalin to conscript them.

'So, I guess it'll have to be another parachute jump, Benjamin.

Last mission, I promise. You'll need to leave the day after tomorrow. We'll look after your dear girl in the meantime.'

Ben found that Kingsley meant that Emma and Jennifer would arrive within days to be on standby as supporters for the birth. Just in case.

In two nights' time, with his backpack ready and his heavily pregnant Annabelle fondly farewelled, Ben boarded his aircraft for another secretive flight over East Germany. Once again, he was on edge for intercepting Russian fighters.

Had he been aware of recent developments east of the border, Ben's heartfelt prayers would have been even more pointed than they already were.

CHAPTER FOURTEEN

'Comrades, are you ready?'

Both Helga Schwarz and her fiancé, Erich, certainly were. The registrar in the Zwickau office was quite matter-of-fact with all the couples who required his time to perform marriage ceremonies, brief and no-frills as they were. He personally regarded marriage as a bourgeois construct, but it was still legal in this developing socialist state, and he was prepared to appease the masses. For a while, of course, until it was finally outlawed.

'Please come forward.' They did.

After outlining the legal requirements, checking the paperwork and getting the young couple's consent to being joined as husband and wife 'for the glories of socialism', he pronounced them married, acknowledging them as such on behalf of the state. It was left to their discretion to kiss, which they did. The bride's older brother was the first to congratulate the happy couple.

'Wonderful, Helga and Erich! I wish you a long and happy life in what will soon be the German Democratic Republic, this socialist paradise!'

Helga received a kiss on the cheek and Erich a firm handshake. Frau Schwarz quietly and discreetly wept where she sat. She was the only one of her family, apart from Reinhard, who was present.

Helga was slightly sorry her other two brothers couldn't be

there. Both had been conscripted by the Wehrmacht for war service. One had died in April 1945, defending Berlin as the Red Army swarmed in to take the capital. Reinhard, part of that onslaught, often wondered if he had engaged his own brother in battle. There was no way of knowing.

The other had been taken prisoner by the invading American forces in Southern Germany. Somehow, she had heard what happened then. 'Reckon this one's good to go. Just a conscript, no evidence of being a Nazi Party member.' The American investigators were happy. So they released him, and he decided to stay in the American zone. Capitalist! He was now a banker in Munich and couldn't visit the Russian zone, even for a wedding. She was unsure if he wanted to, in any case.

They adjourned to a local establishment for a brief reception. Erich had quite a few family members ready to celebrate with the new couple. Following the honeymoon, the newlyweds would be moving away from Zwickau. A larger centre would provide more opportunities.

'Hooray, up it goes!' The obligatory toss of the bridal bouquet, happily caught by Erich's young sister. An omen?

'Herr Schwarz – a phone call.' The waiter nodded in the direction of a private office. Reinhard Schwarz frowned, then responded to the call of duty.

'Yes, Schwarz here.' His mood lightened. 'Well, thank you! I'll come right away. Great news.' He hung up, went out to the reception, which was now coming to an end, and quickly farewelled everybody with a wave, slipping away noiselessly. An unexpected bonus to end a happy event.

The Soviet MGB had arrested a traitor. The enemy operation was about to happen, and he'd pump the man for all he was worth. Finding his car, he headed off in a northerly direction.

Magdeburg, here I come!

- - -

You had to admit this about Reinhard Schwarz. Whatever task he was doing, he did one hundred percent. He would have done it one hundred and fifty percent if it were possible. Analysing successful escapes from the East, a pattern emerged. Secret meetings of discrete groups and organisations. Communication with Western intelligence. Coded messages to guide them to researched weak points in border defences. Shepherding them across to safety in the West, accompanied by their much-valued documents.

'Curse the West and their seductive propaganda!' he yelled out loud.

Then he calmed himself. Losing control was no way to win this Cold War. It was essential to first infiltrate those particular groups to find out when and where they planned their next move.

He asked for and obtained reports from the MGB on likely leads. A good move. The city of Magdeburg had registered increased dissident activity after a quieter period. In fact, it had a lower than average number of successful escapees. That could just be the signal that something big was about to happen.

The MGB was keen to round up the last group that might have information useful to the West and reroute it to Moscow instead. Whatever Special Commissar Schwarz needed, General Volsky ensured he'd have.

'General, first I need your latest border security report identifying any weak points, especially just west of Magdeburg. I need to do some interrogating, so send me your best enforcer as well!'

It was done immediately.

Sitting in a dank MGB cell in Magdeburg Central Prison, Oskar Rittmeyer wondered how they'd got onto him, as he'd done his best to cover his tracks. Perhaps he'd had one too many meetings with his co-conspirators in a semi-public place. Or he'd underestimated the resources and efficiency of the Soviet secret police. They had informers everywhere. It was rumoured the coming German Democratic Republic would establish a similar secret police force to discipline the populace. If so, the GDR would become a frightening place. However, for himself, he was grateful he was no more than a chauffeur. Essentially, he knew nothing.

'Herr Rittmeyer, tell us all you know!' Reinhard Schwarz, as interrogator, liked to open strongly.

Rittmeyer tried to keep back whatever he knew, but most of it came out gradually. Just not his patrons' actual names. They used codenames, he assured Reinhard, but was happy to divulge those.

Reinhard used sleep deprivation over three nights to break Rittmeyer until he had almost everything he needed. The border sector, the number of escapees, if not their actual identities, and the approximate date of the escape bid.

Just one last question. To concentrate Rittmeyer's mind, the Russian enforcer placed a revolver on the table across from him. Reinhard asked it.

'So, who's behind all this? Who's taking them to the West?'

'An Englander! That's all I know. He's done it before!' spat out the terrified chauffeur.

Reinhard looked at his reports. The man spoke the truth. One mentioned scientists from Weimar who went on an excursion west past Gotha and never returned. Police records mentioned a stranger who was with them. Two bus drivers were interviewed and corroborated that story. So, a mysterious Englander! There were also accounts of a torch being flashed from the western side as people escaped the east.

Right, Reinhard would track him down! He'd fix that interloper!

There was nothing more to be gained from Rittmeyer. Reinhard nodded to the Russian enforcer, who picked up his revolver and moved just behind the shaking Rittmeyer, levelling the menacing firearm at the back of his head. The Russian knew the signal. If Reinhard gave the thumbs-down, his victim would be blown to eternity. So far, it had happened every time.

The chauffeur's lips moved in silent prayer. 'Our Father, who art in Heaven...'

Reinhard never knew why he relented. Perhaps because of Rittmeyer's admission about the Englander. Or because his file mentioned he had a young daughter. Reinhard briefly reflected on his own loss of his wife and baby in Leningrad. The Russian was amazed to get the thumbs-up signal. His trembling victim was unexpectedly spared at the last second. He shook his head in disbelief.

'A long spell in jail will sort you out, Rittmeyer! And teach you loyalty to the doctrine of Marxism-Leninism! Take him away!'

Somehow, a jail sentence seemed an utter relief.

CHAPTER FIFTEEN

Ben's night-time parachute descent was no more problematic than last time as he recalled Jock MacTavish's carefully drilled instructions. Blessed with enough moonlight to guide his way to a good landing spot, as before, he hit the ground running and collapsed into his billowing chute, making the landing if not copybook, then at the very least injury-free.

'It's a guid landing if ye kin walk away from it,' as Jock always said. This landing just outside Eilsleben, west of Magdeburg, was good enough.

Scrambling over to a forested area which he'd just avoided, Ben concealed his parachute in thick bushes, packing it down well to avoid discovery. Then, checking his compass, he pointed his torch in the agreed position and flashed it.

No answer. Twice more, he did so. Still no answer.

Whatever had happened to the chauffeur?

There was nothing for it but to move to step two. Walk to the farmhouse, following the directions given. It would be five miles and a risk, given he might encounter Russian patrols because of the closeness of the border. But there was no other option. It was a long trek, but he was fit enough, thanks to his training, footsore nevertheless by the end.

There it was. He knocked at the door. '*Freiheit*.' Would the 'Freedom' code-word be answered?

'*Demokratie,*' came the grateful, correct answer. Yes, Democracy.

He went in. Three expectant pairs of eyes greeted him. Then their owners rose, shaking his hand vigorously. '*Wilkommen, herzlich Wilkommen!*' was their enthusiastic welcome.

'So, where was the chauffeur?' Ben was both annoyed and puzzled.

'We've just heard he's been arrested but didn't have time to walk to the rendezvous to inform you. We hoped you'd jump to step two.'

'Well, I did. Where's the nearest vehicle we can borrow to get to the border?'

No time to lose. These scientists had made their way here from Magdeburg one at a time over three days by various means, one by bus, another by hitchhiking, and the third cadged a lift from a reliable friend. Oskar, the chauffeur, was supposed to meet them here and drive everybody the rest of the way. Sadly, he'd been arrested. Now the clock was definitely ticking.

'There's a farm a kilometre away. Could be a vehicle there.' The disappointed group's only hope.

Ben wracked his brains to remember his course on hot-wiring vehicles for emergency use. Especially those of German make.

'I think the farmer has a pre-war Volkswagen. I noticed when the bus passed there before dropping me here.'

If so, it was a miracle. Ben could 'do' a VW. He'd often practised on one for his course.

'I'll go and check it out.' He had his emergency hot-wiring kit in his pack. Off he went in the recommended direction, praying the farmer didn't have a dog. 'Get ready to leave the moment I come back. It's got to be tonight!'

His prayers were answered. The VW was parked on a slight rise and unlocked. He was able to roll it some distance away, hopefully out of earshot, before using his expertise to get the motor firing gently. Then he drove away as quietly as possible, praying there was plenty of fuel. Half a tank – that would do.

Soon he was back at the farmhouse, and the other three scrambled aboard, two quickly getting into the back. Off they set. Due west to the border. He had previously calculated the distance and checked the topography. The last leg would have to be on foot – it wasn't the sort of border you could normally just drive up to.

'Lieutenant, where exactly will we cross?'

'I know it's a bit of a walk, but we have to find the section less often patrolled by the Russians or communist East Germans. That increases our chances of getting across safely. Once we find the right spot, we'll cross just before dawn when there's a little light. Better than it being pitch-black.'

'We understand.'

Now the Volkswagen was struggling with the uneven terrain, and Ben decided this was it. He parked it in the cover of dense woods, and they got out.

'Shanks's pony from now on!'

'Pardon?'

'We walk!'

They did.

As the night drew on, Ben checked his compass frequently. Yes, they were approaching the desired spot. There was no sign of any Russian guards. There before them was the best place to cross. At least he estimated it was. Whatever moon had been available before had faded. Or was it the dense forest?

They needed the first glimmer of dawn to give them the best chance. With the three fugitives clutching their briefcases stuffed with precious documents and all four quietly waiting back in the shadows, Ben Fletcher checked his watch.

'Half an hour to go.'

Time for some silent prayer.

CHAPTER SIXTEEN

If Reinhard Schwarz had one unfulfilled ambition, it was to become head of state of the coming German Democratic Republic. That position hadn't yet been assigned but the announcement was mere weeks away. Days, practically.

Reinhard burned with ambition and felt one more successful coup would tip the balance in his favour. Personally apprehending a group of scientists fleeing to the West with sensitive nuclear information destined for the GDR's enemies would amount to just such a dazzling success. None of his political rivals who lacked his field experience could boast of anything similar. So he'd steal a march on the lot of them by pulling this one off unaided.

For this reason, he didn't report to General Volsky all the information gleaned from the unfortunate chauffeur, Rittmeyer, but acted on it alone. Hence no Russian troops who could easily have arrested the group were alerted.

Commandeering a vehicle, Reinhard drove towards the disclosed crossing point and lay in wait at what he felt was the exact spot, readying himself in the pitch-blackness. Should they cross in the dark, he had a spotlight. However, his field experience obtained during many battles with the Nazi forces told him they'd wait till just on dawn.

'I'll take out one or two and arrest the others. March them

to the nearest Russian patrol base and confiscate their material. We'll celebrate...!' A simple plan.

Now there was a shaft of light, and he scanned the forest. Movement!

He set up his rifle, ready to command the field of fire, just where they would run down to the barbed wire. He waited. Yes, they were approaching the entanglement and getting ready to go under. Four of them. He wanted to get all four in the frame and take out two with accurate shots. A bullet in the back for those rotten traitors. Now they were getting under the wire...

Reinhard slowly began to squeeze the trigger... just as the tree root he was so carefully balanced on, secretly rotten right through, gave way. His shot, reverberating through the forest, was wildly off-target and hit a nearby tree. He fell awkwardly, losing his firearm, and rolled in the dirt of the forest floor, more annoyed than dazed.

'*Verdammt!*'

'Get under, quick, all of you! Russians!' Ben Fletcher yelled frantically.

They needed no urging. Clutching their briefcases, they made it through to the British side and started sprinting. Stopping to help the least fit German, Ben made up the rear.

On the other side, the frustrated Reinhard picked himself up, regained his rifle and drew a bead on the fleeing group, who were racing to safety on the western side, zigzagging this way and that. They were almost out of range.

He noticed the two stragglers, one almost stumbling. An overfed academic, no doubt. The other must be that cursed Englander! His moment of revenge. Just enough time for a shot.

Reinhard fired. The bullet tore into poor Ben Fletcher's back, just to one side.

'Aargh!' He stumbled and fell. The man he was with and one other some distance in front came back and dragged him to cover, which was fortunately close by. There were no more bullets. They wondered why.

Alerted by the shots, a Russian patrol was nearby, and one of the enlisted men ran up to Reinhard, who was preparing in his fury to blast away at the group seeking cover. His finger was right on the trigger. One more second…

'Comrade, stop! You know our orders. It's forbidden to shoot over the border! We have strict rules. If they get away, good riddance. I'm going to report this!'

An unparalleled act of bravery from a mere unranked soldier before someone of Reinhard's standing. Communism might be a ruthless philosophy, but courageous and honourable men were found everywhere, including Russia. Private Denis Orlov was one of them. He acted without fear or favour.

Frustrated again, Reinhard fired off a string of expletives in Orlov's direction, threw down his firearm and stalked off. He could see this interferer's report landing on General Volsky's desk.

Disaster!

He could kiss his ambitions goodbye.

CHAPTER SEVENTEEN

Crouched in their scant cover just west of the barbed-wire frontier, the desperate group of four waited until they were sure no more shots would come. They used their time to find handkerchiefs to staunch the blood oozing from Ben's wounds. The bullet had exited through his abdomen.

They half dragged, half carried the stricken soldier in the direction of better cover, about fifty metres further on. Two continued to care as best they could for Ben, while the fittest of the three sprinted in the direction of the nearest farmhouse, about three hundred metres away.

'Help, help!' he begged the surprised farmer, who was just getting ready for early morning work. 'We've got a wounded man. Gunshot!'

Living so close to the armed border, the farmer realised the situation immediately, having heard the two distant shots. These weren't the first group of refugees he'd seen who'd passed his farm and certainly wouldn't be the last. Springing into action, he started up his tractor, with a tray attached.

The German scientist balanced on the tray, clinging on for dear life as the farmer sped along as directed. With the tractor screeching to a frantic stop, all involved helped Ben onto the tray, one fugitive lying next to him to keep him still. The others followed along in the direction of the farmhouse, poor

Ben bouncing perilously along. By now, he was lapsing into unconsciousness.

'Kitchen table, best place!' intoned the gruff but kindly farmer.

They carried him inside and stretched him out on the flat surface, hurriedly cleared of everything by the farmer's wife. Frau Wegner rose to the occasion magnificently. Conscripted years before for nursing duty with Hitler's forces, she had forgotten none of her skills, with a stock of bandages and first-aid kit always at the ready. Nursing a Britisher was just the same as one of her own. Ben Fletcher could have asked for nobody more helpful in his hour of need. Even though, by now, he was completely unconscious.

'Peter! Phone Helmstedt for an ambulance. Now!'

Her husband did exactly as ordered. It raced from the nearest town, and Ben was on his way to hospital, with the closest British military post alerted. Next, phone the police to announce the arrival of three unwounded refugees. The astute Wegners knew what to do. Urgent to get them to the police station, then on to the British for interviews. They carried vital material – you could see it in their worried faces.

Helmstedt Hospital was somewhat basic, helpful as the on-site doctor and nurses were. Realising a British serviceman had been shot on duty, the doctor in charge put in a call to Bad Oeynhausen. It went straight through to Colonel Kingsley.

'What, Ben Fletcher shot! We'll send a plane immediately!'

He did.

There were always two transport planes converted to basic air-ambulances fuelled and ready in the allocated hangars, each with a medical team on stand-by. Within minutes, one was airborne, heading for the runway at Helmstedt. For the pilot, a trip in record-breaking time. Then the speediest landing the small town had ever seen.

Wasting not a minute on the retrieval, with the plane continuing to idle on the runway, the medical team plus patient were once again airborne, heading back to base.

'Blood pressure's critically low. Administer medication. Keep up the oxygen.'

They obeyed.

It seemed like hours, but only thirty minutes later, the intercom barked, 'Prepare the patient for landing, we're going in! Headquarters dead ahead.'

Bump. Bump again. Safely down. Sighs of relief.

The entry was as efficient as possible, bearing in mind the patient's condition, now critical. They rushed him into the operating theatre, deathly pale. Units of blood were on standby for an essential transfusion. The senior nurse read Ben's medical details out to the chief surgeon from a clipboard. He'd have to stop the uncontrolled bleeding immediately, that was for sure.

Wasting not a second, he briefed the assembled nurses, the anaesthetist and his assistant surgeon.

'Pray like mad as you work. We'll need a higher power's help to pull this one off!'

They nodded in agreement. Then set to the mammoth task.

Ben Fletcher's life hung by a thread.

- - -

'I'm sorry, love. It's pretty serious!'

Poor Annabelle Fletcher didn't know how to react to her father's terrible news. She burst into tears, then clutched her bulging abdomen as the shock brought on her first labour pain.

'It's started!' Colonel Kingsley was now well and truly out of his depth but had the presence of mind to call in Jennifer and Emma, patiently waiting in the next room. They were already in tears. Now, at least, they had something practical to do by way of supporting Annabelle through the rigours of the hours ahead.

Her bed in the base's small maternity ward was already booked. Once the pains were short-spaced, that was where they'd take Annabelle. For now, it was all about consoling her and concentrating her mind on what lay ahead.

The day before, Myrtle Fletcher had arrived at Kingsley Hall for another visit eagerly arranged by Hermione Kingsley. September was as lovely a month in Oxfordshire as anywhere in England, and the visitor from Surrey wanted to take full advantage of the late summer weather, as well as inspect the latest foal acquired by Kingsley Hall. Not to mention the arranged series of high teas, something Hermione excelled in.

Then, with that terrible phone call from Germany, the boom fell.

'Shot, I can't believe it! And they're operating... Any news?'

Poor Myrtle was inconsolable, and Hermione, as well as the Hall staff, wasn't much better. Myrtle had frightful flashbacks to 1916... news of her poor husband's battlefield death on the Somme... now it was her only son about to suffer the same fate!

'Dear Myrtle, I've phoned Archibald Thompson. He's arranging a prayer service this evening at seven at St Giles. I hope you'll come.'

She would. Anything... Anything.

That evening, sitting in the front pew at St Giles in the exact spot she'd occupied about fifteen months previously for the happy couple's wedding, Myrtle Fletcher lost it completely. The tears wouldn't stop. Rev. Thompson would pause his prayers to come over and console the poor woman, her body wracked with heartfelt sobs. When he wasn't there, Hermione stepped in.

'I can't cope, I just can't cope with this!'

The hearts of all those around her went out to the poor woman. Different members of the congregation, close friends of the Kingsleys and some of the Hall staff, rose from the pews to bring their sincere prayers for Ben's life. Then it was Myrtle's turn.

Drawing on some inner strength to compose herself, she began. She would have to be brief, as she'd lose it again in a minute. She had a flashback to the wedding, the Bible reading and the injunction to 'never give up'. She wouldn't. She just wouldn't!

'Almighty God, I lost my dear husband in battle over thirty

years ago, and now I may lose my only child, my son Ben, grievously wounded in his country's service. Please, in your mercy, spare him! Spare him!'

She collapsed again into the pew, sobbing uncontrollably for five minutes as many left their seats to comfort the distressed mother.

Then a strange thing happened.

A calmness came over the assembled gathering.

Rev. Thompson was the first to notice it, then others. An unseen force was comforting everyone, soothing their fears. They just couldn't explain it.

Suddenly, Myrtle Fletcher stopped crying altogether and looked around, her eyes now dry. Yes, she knew. A decision had been made in a higher place, and her frantic, desperate prayer was answered. A wonderful, merciful decision. Brightly, she got up and addressed everyone.

'Don't worry, everybody. Ben's going to live!'

You just can't explain faith like that.

- - -

Exactly one minute before the prayer meeting was concluded, the intensive care ward nurse in charge of supervising the moribund patient was sadly waiting for him to draw his last breath.

The operation had technically been a success. His left kidney, which had taken the full force of the bullet, was so shattered it just had to be removed. But other organs, while still more or less intact, had lost so much blood that his poor body was giving up the ghost.

They had given him as much in the way of transfusions as he needed, and had pumped in copious amounts of medication, so there was really nothing more they could do. Once his shallow breathing ceased and there was no pulse, the nurse would cover his face with the sheet and call the doctor to certify the time of death. This watch was the saddest one of all.

How she hated the death watch.

'Was that it?' she wondered. 'His last breath?' Her hand touched the sheet. Well, check the pulse first.

As she went to do so, Nurse Parker noticed a flicker in one eyelid. Followed by the other. Then his breathing started back again.

Yes, he was alive!

'Doctor, Doctor! He's alive! Come quickly!'

The doctor couldn't believe it. In the tearoom, he had been chatting to colleagues, preparing himself for the final certification, saying he'd never seen anyone with such injuries and blood loss come back from the dead.

'Not a chance in a million, I'll lay you odds. So sad. That poor blighter doesn't have an earthly. If he makes it, I'll eat my hat!'

Minutes later, with Ben Fletcher breathing strongly and now coming back to consciousness, the doctor returned to his astonished colleagues.

'Mates, throw some tomato sauce on my surgical cap! I've got chewing to do. Then come and meet the man in a million!'

Ben Fletcher was back.

'Push! Go on, one more push will do it!' both the doctor and nurse urged poor Annabelle.

They were right, and the baby was delivered. Her ordeal, relieved by the administration of gas as often as she clamoured for it, with ice dropped regularly into her mouth by either Emma or Jennifer, was over at last. A bouncing baby boy, very healthy.

'If Ben dies, he'll take his name. Otherwise, I really don't know.'

Now, with the childbirth over, she once again turned her attention to the other trauma. Was she a widow? The very idea was too much to bear. Wisely, all those present concentrated her thoughts on the new baby, cooing in delight at how handsome he was and how healthy. A fine young man. If the worst came to the worst, he would be a wonderful consolation. She remembered that, over thirty years previously, dear Myrtle was in exactly the same situation. With a fatherless son.

As the worried Annabelle cuddled her newborn, with Emma and Jennifer not quite knowing what to do next, there was a sudden knock at the door. A nurse.

'Congratulations, Mrs Fletcher, on your son. I have a wheelchair here. Would you like me to wheel you both up to intensive care to meet his father?'

'What, Ben's alright? You mean he's alive?'

'He certainly is. And asking to see you both. Ready now?'

All three women shrieked and screamed with delight. Baby Fletcher must have wondered what a strange world he'd been born into.

Poor Nurse Parker was deaf for the rest of her shift.

CHAPTER EIGHTEEN

'Well, old boy, like the Battle of Waterloo, it was a near-run thing!' It had been a rushed plane flight from Berlin to Ben's hospital ward, but Horace Kingsley had made it in record time.

Trust the old colonel to use a military analogy. It was appropriate and accurate.

'Yes, sir, I agree. I've never been through anything like it. The arm wound in France was a picnic in comparison.' True enough. It would be a while till Ben regained full strength.

'What are we going to do with you? You've been well and truly compromised east of the border. No more missions for you. Especially now you and Annie have the little one. By the way, we've found out you were shot by a rogue East German, not the Russians. Some communist bucking for promotion or the like. He'd used secret police methods to lie in wait for your group and intended to assassinate the lot of you. Make his reputation and guarantee his future. That sort of thing. So, have you had a think?'

'Yes. Annie and I have had a talk and made our decision.'

'Which is?'

'Because of the baby, she's now out of the workforce indefinitely. As for me, I'll retire from the army and Military Intelligence. Ten years is enough!'

'Fine, I'll do the paperwork for your demobbing. For

meritorious service, you've been promoted to captain. That'll increase your pension. You've earned it!'

'Thank you, sir.'

'Don't mention it.'

With that, once fully recovered by late autumn, Ben and Annabelle, plus their baby son named James, left Germany and were en route back to the Old Dart. He was minus a kidney but otherwise back to good health.

They never ceased to give thanks for his miraculous recovery. Nor did Myrtle Fletcher.

- - -

The flat in Cranleigh was a slight anticlimax after the hurly-burly of Germany, but life there was pleasant enough. They lived around the corner from Myrtle, and Ben tried a security job, trying to remember what sort of work he'd undertaken prior to joining the army in 1939. That seemed ages ago. The service gave him a free occupational assessment and determined he had an aptitude for business. That suited him fine, but what he tried led only to dead ends.

They received good news in late 1950. Annabelle was pregnant again. This time, she felt it would be a daughter. Great, a pigeon pair. A lovely sister for young James, who was as healthy a toddler as you could wish for. As they anticipated the birth, one thought kept recurring.

'Annie, how about we emigrate after the baby comes? England seems too small for us.'

'I'd love to. Greener pastures. There are plenty of other places to raise a family.'

'My mum has your family to support her up in Kingsley Hall so she'll be properly looked after. In any case, she's welcome to visit often. Or join us, if she'd prefer. We'll help her migrate, too, if she wants.'

Four Commonwealth countries were actively seeking

immigrants. Any one would suit them. Each nation had a High Commission in London, and they visited the four, collecting brochures and application forms. Canada, South Africa, Australia and New Zealand were eager to entice migrants and produced their own spiel. The couple considered them all thoroughly. Ben thought back to the Berlin airlift and the camaraderie he'd enjoyed with the various crews. They had something special, the lot of them.

Canada – the second largest country on earth, spread over how many time zones? Any province would be an ideal home, although possibly not the frozen north. Alberta especially appealed, and they could see themselves somewhere such as Calgary, or maybe Edmonton, the provincial capital. Or they could try Vancouver in British Columbia, or Victoria on the island just to the west. For the east, there were great possibilities in Toronto, for example, or Montreal. A go-ahead, bilingual nation worthy of consideration. Go, Canada!

South Africa – a temperate, sunny climate. Main languages English and Afrikaans. Cape Town or Johannesburg might be obvious destinations. Should they try farming on the veldt or launch into wine production somewhere such as the picturesque region of Stellenbosch? Ben had always thrilled to the story of Mafeking and Lord Baden Powell. Was that location a possibility? They studied the brochures carefully. Nestled in the far reaches of the continent, South Africa would give them a prosperous future and had its attractions.

Australia – one of the two farthest away. A vast continent whose remoteness could be an advantage. Wonderful capital cities of each state, with the Northern Territory a type of frontier as a possible choice. Like South Africa, much of the continent had a temperate climate, although there was a tropical north, should that entice them. A vast outback, seemingly continuing forever. Australia was a definite option. Brisbane? Sydney? Melbourne? Or Hobart, Adelaide and Perth as charming alternatives.

Finally, New Zealand – the 'antipodes', exactly the opposite point on the globe from the United Kingdom. A fertile, green and partly mountainous country, compact in area but high in quality. Very British in its outlook. A laid-back lifestyle and, because of its location, very much 'away from it all'. Auckland, Wellington or Christchurch would be great for a city life, otherwise there were many rural locations that would suit. North Island or South? They certainly loved the look of those mountains. New Zealand exerted its pull.

'Too much to consider for now. Definitely later.' They put all of this on the back burner until after the baby came. Ben was going to be around this time!

Annabelle's prediction came to pass. A healthy daughter, a real delight. Ben was chuffed to be allowed to stay during the first stage of labour and wait outside for the actual birth. Somehow, this one was easier. After a week in hospital, it was time to bring mother and baby home.

In their Cranleigh flat, which was now somewhat more crowded, the couple got out the migration brochures once more and evaluated all the pros and cons of the four prospective countries. Each was stunning in its own individual way, but they'd have to make a choice. A couple with a young family, the Fletchers would be excellent prospects anywhere.

One Sunday afternoon, they did a final list check and decided each would write down their choice secretly before revealing it to the other. They did so.

Wow, they'd chosen the same country for much the same reasons! The next day, they lodged the paperwork and waited. Not for too long. They were accepted and ship's passage reserved.

Their family farewell party was held in Kingsley Hall at the end of January amid tears of both joy and regret. Both families would miss them terribly but promised to visit, as did Ben and Annabelle in return. Apart from the usual parting gifts, Colonel Kingsley had one extra for Ben. He discreetly asked the servants to retire just before dessert was served.

'I can't give you a copy, but this report details the benefit the

United Kingdom received from the papers brought over by the various technicians and scientists you helped smuggle over the border. Especially the last mission which almost killed you.'

Ben winced. His left kidney area would never be one hundred percent recovered. How grateful he was his right kidney was working at full efficiency and was likely to do so for life.

'Yes, thanks to your courage, our nuclear program is well on track. It'll help provide an effective counterbalance to the Soviet Union. The free world owes you a great debt.'

'I just did my bit, sir.'

'The prime minister has sent this medal in acknowledgement and authorised me to award it. Still a bit hush-hush, you know. Family – that includes you.' Everybody laughed but knew he was in earnest. This was for the family's eyes and knowledge only.

Ben blushed, took the report, flicked through it and handed it back. Then held up the medal. They gave him three cheers. He blushed again.

'Well, that's it. Dessert is served.' The servants returned to do so.

Thus was Ben's official retirement from Military Intelligence. A night to remember.

- - -

With a great deal of hooting, tooting and constant blasting from the funnel, the *Arcadia* pulled away from the wharf in Portsmouth, the streamers held both by the hands of the passengers and their family and friends on the wharf straining until they tore, floating behind the departing ship like octopus tentacles until they, too, were swallowed up in the maelstrom created by the ship's powerful propeller.

Standing on the deck in their huge winter overcoats that blustery, freezing February day in 1952, Ben and Annabelle waved to their family and friends on the wharf. Waved almost until their arms were sore. But England was receding on the horizon, the ship heading into the Channel and then the

Atlantic before setting its course towards their destination, their future home.

'A new adventure, son,' he said to his toddler standing beside him, who was similarly rugged up. Young James nodded, appreciating something of what lay before them, although far too young to register its import.

Annabelle stood next to Ben, cradling their baby daughter. They had swapped holding her during their frantic waving to family and friends on the wharf, but now she reposed comfortably in Annabelle's encompassing arms. A loving family anticipating the next stage in life's adventure.

'Paper, sir and madam?' One of the solicitous stewards interrupted their reverie. A timely interruption, as they were already thinking about leaving the winter chill of the deck to retire to their cabin.

'Thank you.'

It was a momentous day in more ways than one. They read the tragic headline, '*King Dies*'. Then the subheading – '*Princess Elizabeth to Take Throne*'. That day was indeed the end of an era and the beginning of a new one.

Annabelle had her own thoughts on it. 'I reckon she'll do well. Elizabeth's got spirit.'

The new queen was flying back from Kenya, her planned world tour with her husband sadly interrupted. Ben, knowing Princess Elizabeth's war record and service to her country from the moment she was old enough to volunteer, agreed.

'She'll leave her mark. I predict the new monarch will have a long reign ahead of her. The United Kingdom's in good hands.'

As they prepared to leave the spot and find their cabin, Ben stopped them. With one hand, he made a sweeping gesture in the direction of the Continent, and with the other gently patted each child on the head.

'At least they'll live their lives far from the cares of Europe!'

On that score, time would tell.

Bergen-Belsen camp

Memorial stone

Occupation zones

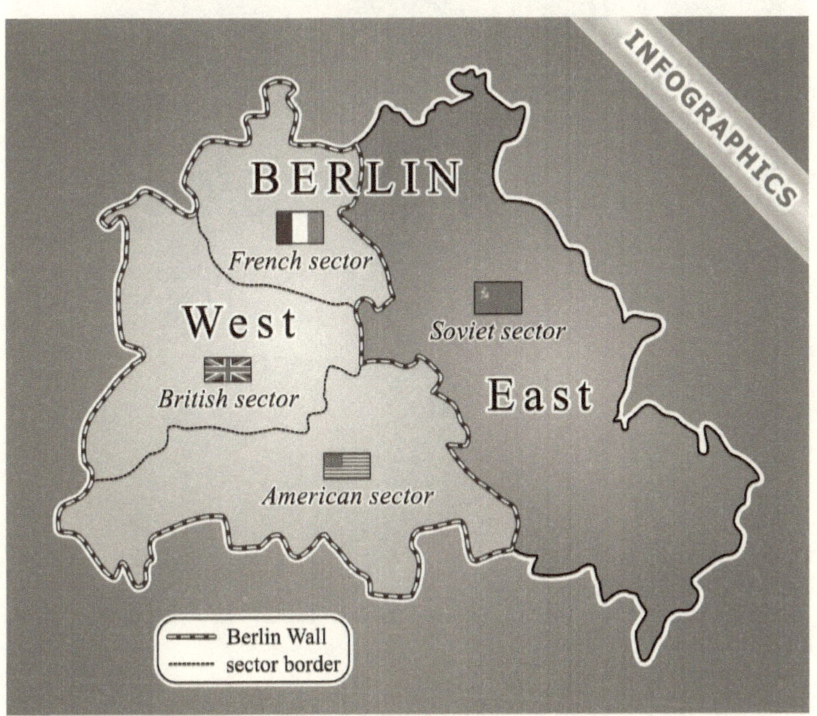

Divided Berlin

YOU ARE LEAVING
THE AMERICAN SECTOR
ВЫ ВЫЕЗЖАЕТЕ ИЗ
АМЕРИКАНСКОГО СЕКТОРА
VOUS SORTEZ
DU SECTEUR AMERICAIN
SIE VERLASSEN DEN AMERIKANISCHEN SEKTOR
hmühlenstraße
493

Berlin

East German border fence

Brandenburg Gate

PART TWO

CHAPTER ONE

The worst of the northern winter was now receding, as evidenced by a quick glance from the office window. Signs of spring emerging in the carefully manicured gardens below were considered a good omen, especially by this notably superstitious man.

Otto Dreschner had deliberately chosen today, Tuesday 15 March 1983, to unveil his master plan. He congratulated himself on his personal knowledge as he, a proud student of history, thought back to the significance of the Ides of March on that faraway date back in 44 BC when Julius Caesar was murdered.

Would his plan involve an assassination? Dreschner smiled to himself as he considered the thought. Nothing was beyond him.

During the last few days, the head of the German Democratic Republic's professionally named Main Directorate for Reconnaissance had worked feverishly to put together his project. A significant branch of the State Security Service, generally known as the Stasi, the Directorate was responsible for espionage conducted abroad. A job Dreschner relished. His aim was to make his country, East Germany, pre-eminent in the world. Far-fetched? Maybe, but he was utterly determined. His name derived from 'a thresher', and that was how he served his country. Threshing the population to drive out traitors.

'Got everything?' he mused to himself as he gathered his papers and other material, before walking the short distance down the corridor to the meeting room. He glanced at his wristwatch – 9.25 a.m. Showtime would be in five minutes.

Stasi headquarters were in Lichtenberg, a suburb of East Berlin, capital of the GDR, the Stalinist offspring of the former Soviet zone of occupation in Eastern Germany. West of the border, it faced the Federal Republic, free and truly democratic rather than being a satellite of the Soviet Union. For the GDR, the title 'Democratic' was almost a cruel joke, emphasised by the predominance of the Stasi, with its secret police and network of informers. No wonder they had to build the Berlin Wall to keep people from fleeing to the West.

'Good morning, comrades!'

As Dreschner entered the meeting room, all but one stood to greet him and reply to his salutation. The exception, confined by rank to his chair, was Horst Moltke, overall chief of the Stasi, coordinator of the various units. The one person present who was Dreschner's superior. Yet, once the Stasi flag was unfurled, he too stood to acknowledge it.

'Comrades,' Dreschner began, 'it's time to unveil our master plan. As you are aware, our agents have been quietly at work in various posts abroad, but now it's essential to concentrate on the target area. An event that occurred precisely ten days ago has the potential to bring our superb workers' paradise into the winners' circle. Some of you may be aware of it.'

A curious murmur of voices proved that few, in fact, knew where he was going. Dreschner alone had been in contact with a particular overseas embassy to glean the necessary facts.

'To tip the balance in favour of both the GDR and our glorious ally, the Soviet Union, we must strike where the enemy, the West, least expects it. In this way, our democratic forces can win the Cold War and dominate the West. Preferably without firing a shot!'

'Do tell, Comrade Dreschner!'

'Please, let me continue. The election of a potentially... shall we say *malleable* government in the target area puts the GDR in a position to bring our plans to a climax. I wish to now reveal our seven-year plan for world domination on the coattails of the great Soviet Union. In short, we'll put our ally in the box seat by turning the tables on the West!'

One of Dreschner's comrades wasn't nearly as convinced as he was. 'How so, comrade? The Soviets are losing patience with us because of the expense of maintaining their army here in the GDR. There's even talk of them pulling out. We're under constant pressure to contribute to the Warsaw Pact and provide a viable alternative to the seduction of the West.'

'Precisely! When my plan succeeds, it'll turn things round completely. No longer will we be seen as a client state but an equal partner. Comrade Moltke knows I've run my plan past the Russian KGB and they approve!' The mention of the latest version of the Soviet secret service was enough to get their attention.

Horst Moltke nodded in agreement. Dreschner indeed had been burning the midnight oil these last few days.

'Well, let's concentrate on the target. The moles we planted are ready to be activated. Some have been quietly working away for years but, under the last conservative government there, were unable to expand their activities. That has now changed. So it's time to move. Seven years to glory!'

They practically cheered him. Dreschner knew his time had come. He'd be head of the Stasi once Moltke retired, which would surely happen in the next few years. Yes, he was prepared to bide his time. More than that, this coming success would set him up for life. He'd be a famous socialist hero...

Dreschner snapped back to reality.

'Now, the exact details. Our target has been always a Western ally and is presently firmly in that camp with a long-standing alliance with the USA. Our agents – moles, it's true – are now in a position to influence government policy, then bring about radical change, and... well, you can guess the rest. Standard operating procedure! All in solidarity with the Soviet Union.

Don't worry, our embassy in the target capital is already working to that end!'

'Well done, comrade!'

Dreschner glowed with appreciation. 'The Soviet Union is poised to enter that part of the world and dominate it. They're ready to build up their forces in expectation, so the KGB inform me. The payoff for the GDR is that, with the West then weakened after what amounts to a coup, we can expand and take over West Germany! Socialism for all of Germany, not just our state!'

There was a collective intake of breath. They were on the edge of their chairs.

'Mark your calendars, comrades. I offer you Code 1990. In seven years, there will be a combined state of Germany. Under our banner!'

'So, where will we strike?'

As the finale to his grand show, Dreschner moved over to the large world globe on a nearby table and gave it a spin. As an omen, it stopped right where he expected, and he dramatically tapped the spot.

Australia.

CHAPTER TWO

The Stasi had really begun to raise the profile of Australia as part of their world aims at the time of the election of the Whitlam government in 1972. Somehow, they felt a Labor government would give far more traction than a conservative one.

Their plans were temporarily put on ice when Whitlam fell three years later. Curse that conservative coup! However, with Labor now in power, likely for years, the time had come.

Once back in his office, Otto Dreschner reviewed his voluminous file on his target's new government. The embassy in Canberra had been most helpful. There they were. Prime Minister Robert James Lee Hawke. Deputy Lionel Bowen. Treasurer Paul Keating. Next, Brian Howe... the list went on.

Back to more on Bob Hawke, as they called him. The man had cleverly persuaded colleagues to depose the former party leader, Bill Hayden, as he himself was a certainty to be elected. President of a confederation of unions, the Australian Council of Trade Unions, for about eleven years, a member of parliament for only about two and a half years. Yes, Hawke was on the ladder of success for sure. Plenty of ambition...

'Well, what's his take on Foreign Affairs?' Dreschner wondered. 'Let's see. Fancy, Bill Hayden has been appointed Minister for Foreign Affairs. How will that work out?'

He read on. The embassy confirmed Hawke was an enthusiastic

supporter of the US alliance and would no doubt do his best to convince any waverers in his party – and there'd be plenty – to toe the line there.

'Oh, we'll break the ANZUS Alliance, give us time!' was Dreschner's petulant response as he flung the paper down. He was aware from intelligence briefings New Zealand was now about to react to visits by nuclear-armed ships. A good start, but lots more to do… That US alliance, a defence linking of the three nations, had to be ruptured. He had exactly the means to do it.

If Otto Dreschner had been honest with himself, he would have admitted the Australian government of Prime Minister Bob Hawke, elected on 5 March, was no more likely to be influenced by the wiles of East Germany than the previous conservative one of Malcolm Fraser. The timetable was more a personal one. Nevertheless, Dreschner was determined to make it work. Nineteen ninety was to be a year of destiny. Yes, his personal destiny!

Code 1990 was locked in.

Dreschner reflected on his life so far.

Aged forty-five, he still had plenty of useful career ahead of him. Born the year before the war in a village just north of Berlin, he had grown up in the capital of his country knowing nothing other than the communist doctrine, which he had enthusiastically adopted. He had joined the Stasi as a junior officer after a period of military service, then quickly rose through the ranks. Married to Brunhilde, just as eager a communist as he was, he had two children.

As to further advancement: Moltke's job would suit him just fine. After that, once the present operation succeeded, his reputation would be made… Chancellor of a united, socialist Germany?

No sooner had the meeting ended than he returned to his office and contacted someone who'd been groomed for his particular role for months, one Klaus Ziegler, a resident of Bonn in West Germany. Some distance beyond the barbed-wire, fortified border that separated the two parts of what had once been a unified nation.

'Klaus, time to visit the Australian Embassy and put in your application. Get all your papers together, but don't rush it. Check all's in order – it's OK to take a few months to get there if you need to. We're taking the long view here. You'll need to bone up on more course information to establish credibility for your coming university study. We'll be aiming for a start in their next academic year, anyway.'

'Very good, sir. I was expecting your call. I'll make the appointment right away.'

'Comrade, I know I can depend on you!'

Indeed he could. Dreschner had Ziegler's file in front of him, the facts neatly laid out.

Born in 1953 in Dresden to parents who had embraced the philosophy of the GDR from the beginning of its formation. Schooled through the various socialist youth groups he'd joined. Identified in his high school days as a potential Stasi recruit. Meritorious national service followed by a further stint in the army. Significantly, great enthusiasm for the work of the Stasi, to whose membership he was then recommended. Eagerness to hunt down resisters of the regime. Obedience to orders without question. A firm belief in the coming dominance of communism.

'An ideal officer!' Dreschner happily acknowledged.

As he hung up, Dreschner certainly knew the calibre of the man, well-schooled in his role. He reflected on Ziegler's training. It took place in a special camp in the country's south-west, in a secluded forest area set up with different sections, each a replica of the foreign nation the agents would be posted to.

So, for Ziegler, the 'Australia' camp featured regular deliveries of local newspapers, news bulletins, posters of different geographical features. Ayers Rock, the Great Barrier Reef, Rottnest Island, the Twelve Apostles, Tasmania's Cradle Mountain, Mount Gambier, the Sydney Opera House – it was a travel bonanza.

Ziegler had immersed himself in watching videotapes of Australian television shows, especially political broadcasts from the ABC. A perfect cover for his planned study of a Master of Political Science at the University of Sydney. However, his 'politics' would be of a wholly different nature… Practical, you might say.

One feature of Australian life that really tickled his fancy was horse racing. Time and again, he watched videotapes of races such as the Melbourne Cup, then learned the basics of betting. He was unsure if this was in concert with the expectations of socialism. Perhaps it was the forbidden fruit aspect of it that appealed. He made a mental note to follow it up once 'down under'. A terrific cover.

'Congratulations, Comrade Ziegler. You've now graduated!'

Otto Dreschner had visited him when that part of his training was complete. Ziegler was then, as it were, spirited over the border to West Germany to await his mission. The Stasi was quite adept in providing false papers to show Ziegler was, in fact, a resident of the West and quite free to move to whatever country he wished. In this case, to become an overseas student in Australia.

His life had been one excitement after another, thanks to the benefits he'd received from his Stasi benefactors. Very intelligent and thoroughly devoted to his country's philosophy, Ziegler had a definite bent for espionage. All in the service of the GDR, of course. He was as keen as any other young man to find a wife but, so far, hadn't met any woman who quite shared his political ardour. Hopefully, that would come later. For now, it was all about the coming mission. When the details became clear during his training in the forest camp, his enthusiasm was palpable.

Now he'd been given the go-ahead and it was time to move.

As Klaus Ziegler, papers in hand and ready for his appointment, walked up to the Australian Embassy, he couldn't repress a frisson of excitement.

'Australia – I'm on the way!'

CHAPTER THREE

The East German regime had been a brutal one right from its inception, enforced by an occupying Soviet army. Paranoid about resisters, once the Stasi was set in place, it established a network of informers, causing many citizens to be arrested and convicted on spurious charges, all under the heading of 'resistance to the regime'. This resulted in a large number of attempted escapes to the West, hence the necessary erection of a barbed-wire border to prevent this, plus the organisation of a force of military guards to apprehend or kill the many would-be escapees.

One outlet was free passage between Soviet-occupied East Berlin and the Western sectors. Free West Berlin was an island of hope deep within East German territory. However, with the erection of a wall around West Berlin in August 1961, that freedom was immediately cut off.

In order to raise an effective military force, the National People's Army was established in 1956, then in 1962, conscription became compulsory for all GDR males at age eighteen, requiring an eighteen-month service. Some of these were allocated to the Grenztruppen, the Border Troops. With desperate people just waiting their chance, there was much for them to do.

Nineteen-year-old Gregor Laube, a resident of Karl-Marx-Stadt, the former Chemnitz, had been conscripted for just such duty in 1971. Now, the following summer, he was patrolling the allocated border sector in his country's far south-west.

Sudden movement from the bushes!

He was on to them. His submachine gun was cocked and ready.

Gregor had received the usual indoctrination during his high school education and supported the aims of the GDR... or, at least, did so until recently. If not rostered for duty on Sundays, he was a regular attender of the nearest Lutheran Church in the small town of Eisenach. That was at least one concession from the atheistic regime. It was hardly encouraged but believers could attend church if they insisted.

He had to admit part of the attraction was Pastor Kasner's attractive eighteen-year-old daughter, Angela, who had so far resisted any brief overtures he'd made. The Kasners weren't from this part of East Germany but had come down from Templin, further north, to fill a temporary vacancy. Angela was in high school there but was here for the summer holidays. Gregor did his best to concentrate on the sermons, yet Angela was a constant distraction...

But back to duty – yes, two trying to flee – a man and a woman...

'Halt! Halt!' This would be the only warning he'd give.

They only ran faster and were now almost at the barbed wire, which might allow just enough room underneath for desperadoes to chance it. Gregor took aim... One burst would take them out, and they'd be two more kill notches on the board back in the barracks. He'd be 'blooded', just like the others.

An unseen force made him hesitate.

Last Sunday, Pastor Kasner's message was clearly *'Thou Shalt Not Kill!'* In other words, *'Don't Commit Murder!'* What was he about to do? Kill two people who were doing him no harm and only wanted to escape. Yes, they were breaking the law, but did that justify killing unarmed refugees? The mental debate continued. Man's law or God's law? Man's law or God's law?

God won.

Gregor moved his weapon up and fired over their heads, shattering a couple of tree branches and terrifying a pair of birds, which flew off, squawking.

Urged on, the couple threw themselves in desperation under the barbed wire, wriggling frantically until they got through to the other end. The last Gregor saw of them, they were running fit to burst, zigzagging their way to proper cover on the West German side, no doubt frightened out of their wits in case there was another burst of fire...

'*Du Weichei!*' Gregor's sergeant screamed. 'You wimp!'

He ran up to the hapless conscript, knocking him flying in his fury. 'You idiot, you had a clear shot! Those damned refugees got clear away!'

As Gregor staggered to his feet, nursing a sore body, the apoplectic sergeant went on, 'Right, nincompoop, you're fined a month's pay. Turn in your weapon and report for kitchen duty from now till lights out. I'll fix you, Laube! Get out of my sight!'

The rest of the day wasn't a happy memory for Gregor. His enforced duty eventually over, he gratefully collapsed in his barracks bed, nursing both a sore body and aching wrists from hour after hour of potato peeling, and fervently prayed for a good night's rest. As he soon drifted off, knowing his prayer was answered, he saw the kindly face of Pastor Kasner, nodding approvingly. He also imagined Angela doing likewise. His conscience was clear...

That night, Private Gregor Laube enjoyed the best sleep of his life.

CHAPTER FOUR

Desperate for cover and now entirely breathless, the couple collapsed behind a group of trees once they realised how blessed they had been to make it through to the sanctuary of the Federal Republic of Germany – the West! Free at last!

'We made it, Ursula! I don't know how we weren't shot, but we got through! I thought we were done for!' Jonas Schneider embraced his wife in gratitude. Once they had somewhat recovered, the search was on to find a local and report their arrival.

Each clutching their only possession, a small suitcase, they spied a farmhouse about three hundred metres away and made their way towards it. The farmer saw them first and rushed to greet them, realising where they'd come from. The inevitable scratches from their frantic dash under the barbed wire were a dead giveaway.

'Welcome to the West! Would you like a cup of tea?' The question seemed surreal.

'Anything, please! We were almost shot and need to regroup. Now, contact the police so we can report our escape!'

'Sure, but come inside and relax. I'll phone them in a minute. Tell me your story over a cup of tea – or I've got a medicinal schnapps, if that will help.'

They gratefully agreed.

Over refreshments, having been provided some basic first aid for their wounds, Jonas and Ursula revealed the motivation for their desperate escape. As a teacher of mechanical engineering at the University of Leipzig, he had been denounced to the Stasi by a student informer. The man's motivation had simply been that he had failed an assignment and was due to repeat a semester.

With the word out from colleagues he was on the Stasi arrest list, both he and Ursula, a kindergarten teacher, made the critical decision to try to escape to the West. And here, by an amazing turn of circumstance, they were!

A knock on the door signified two police had arrived to take their particulars.

Farewelling the kind farmer – they weren't the first refugees to find sanctuary there – the Schneiders were driven to the local police station for an interview then on to the nearest refugee centre for processing. By the time they fell asleep that night in a hostel bed, dreaming of their new life to come, Jonas and Ursula were absolutely exhausted.

What a day! What a miracle!

- - -

The Schneiders were placed on a well-oiled process line for their new life in the West. With evidence of their qualifications, there were jobs available for this enterprising couple in their mid-thirties. Relocated to the city of Essen, far from the troubled border with the East, Jonas found a lecturing position at one of the universities, allowing him to do further research in his field. Ursula had no trouble obtaining work as a kindergarten teacher.

However, as time went by, they developed itchy feet and felt Europe was too small for them. It was a wide world out there! They improved their basic knowledge of English, seeing it as a passport to a better life. Newspaper advertisements encouraged them to seek wider opportunities.

'Hey, Ursula! See this ad for a position in Australia! The University of New South Wales in Sydney – you know, the

Opera House city.' They had heard about the opening of that edifice by Queen Elizabeth two years ago, in 1973.

'Sure, I'm up for it. Why not apply? I'm keen to start writing children's books. Maybe I could start with some of those Australian animals and birds. Great Gertie Goanna? That's got a nice ring to it.'

So Jonas applied. Surprise – he got the job offer as a lecturer in mechanical engineering, his specialty.

The Australian Embassy in Bonn was very helpful indeed. With confirmed work available in Sydney, the Schneiders soon had migration approval and were on their way.

Farewell, Europe.

Following their long Qantas flight from Frankfurt and arrival in their new country, they spent a week in a Sydney hotel, giving them time to get to know the city. Then the university settlement officer arranged a flat in nearby Kensington with a year's lease. An orientation meeting with Jonas's colleagues, who were eager to learn of his precise German slant on their academic discipline, made the couple immediately feel at home. The Aussies did their best to put them at ease.

Just one thing made them smile. A curious thing, the Australian brand of humour!

CHAPTER FIVE

It was a stunning spring day in September 1983 when Klaus Ziegler, aka the Ringmaster, slipped into Sydney. He couldn't help but admire the fruits of capitalism, despite himself.

That day, the whole country was agog with Australia's win from behind in the America's Cup with its space-age winged-keel yacht. Ziegler grudgingly preferred America to go down rather than his target, Australia, but was beside himself seeing on television Prime Minister Hawke – Bob Hawke – urge workers to take the day off! That would be unthinkable in the GDR!

Just what sort of leader did this place have?

Days before, he'd been fondly wished a secret bon voyage by Otto Dreschner, with full instructions as to the unfolding of Mission Southern Cross, as it was termed. Link up with the moles who had been planted in Australia years before and activate them. One was now a member of parliament in Western Australia, unbelievably. He'd migrated years before and had anglicised his name. Another was head of an influential industrial union based in a town north of Sydney. They'd have important work to discuss. Then organise what would follow...

Back in East Germany, Otto Dreschner felt his destiny was on track and couldn't resist confiding in Brunhilde, who he knew to be completely loyal. And discreet.

'Yes, 1990 will be my year, mark my words. My astrologer confirmed it.'

His wife was unsure if consulting an astrologer was in line with communist doctrine but knew better than to contradict her husband. Besides, powerful men in whatever system of government often make their own rules. Communism was no exception.

'A clairvoyant genius, he's given me a mock-up of the 1990 calendar with significant dates circled.' Dreschner could see it all now. The West in retreat, and the Soviet Union in control. As a payoff, all Germany united under a socialist banner. Himself as chancellor! A glorious future, indeed!

Brunhilde gave him a kiss and then left her husband to his speculations…

For Klaus Ziegler, having found accommodation in Glebe, close to the University of Sydney, where he would be enrolled, there was now an essential appointment to set up his cover. He wasn't one to arouse suspicion by unnecessary delay.

The very week of his arrival, he made his way the short distance into the city to No. 95 Gascoyne Street, the headquarters annexe of the Commonwealth Department of Immigration, where he presented himself for an interview. It was essential for officers of that department to approve the study plans of overseas students in the category Ziegler had nominated.

Kendrick Findlay was the head of the department's foreign study division located in the annexe and delighted in personally interviewing prospective master's degree students, leaving the lesser applicants to other staff. He'd schedule any time in the week for this, apart from a Wednesday afternoon, his regular golf game. Findlay would have been shocked had he realised that not only did the Stasi know of his existence, but they had a file on him. Dreschner's tentacles reached everywhere.

Findlay was a dedicated member of the Australian Labor Party and an office-bearer in his suburban branch, Penshurst. Ziegler had a summary of the file and had deduced that a thesis topic sympathetic to Findlay's left-leaning philosophy would be most likely to gain approval, should there be any doubt. He didn't want some government official being in a position to veto his mission. Thus, his plan went swimmingly...

'Well, Mr Ziegler, everything seems good. I compliment you on having your paperwork in meticulous order. I see you will soon be undertaking a bridging course just up the road at the University of Sydney, then enrolling there in your Master of Political Science at the start of 1984. Do you have any aims of further study beyond your master's?'

'Yes, I intend to go on to a PhD as a follow-up and hope to be in Australia for quite a while. It's a great country!'

'Sure, glad you feel happy here. I approve of your master's research topic, *"Immigrants and their Attachment to Australian Democracy Across the Political Spectrum"*. In fact, I'd love to read it when it's published.' In somewhat of an aside, he went on, 'Just between you and me, I'm a bit political myself...!' Findlay winked.

'Really, sir? I wouldn't have guessed!' Ziegler lied, being practically able to recite the section head's Stasi file off by heart.

'Thank you, Mr Ziegler. I'll inform the minister you're approved and all's good. *Auf Wiedersehen* for now!' Kendrick Findlay liked his little touch.

'Goodbye, Mr Findlay. Or, as you say, *auf Wiedersehen*. I compliment you on your command of German.' Ziegler could play it any way the locals wanted. Left-leaning member of the ALP? Still cursed capitalists.

He'd fix them.

Stage One nicely completed. Next stop, Sydney Uni.

The Ringmaster was on his way.

CHAPTER SIX

Otto Dreschner had laid his groundwork carefully, years before. Following training in the forest camp deep in his country's south-west, nominated agents had been ferreted into West Germany, where they applied for migration papers through the Australian Embassy in Bonn. With Australia always on the lookout for skilled migrants, especially from Western Europe, it was easy for the agents – destined to be moles – to slip into Australia and obtain permanent residency, even citizenship. No problem at all. All they then had to do was await their opportunity. Which the Ringmaster would provide.

Thus it was Ernst Richter, a competent tradesman, entered Australia through Perth in the late 1960s. A fitter and machinist, he obtained work there and soon joined his local branch of the ALP. Making it his business to be friendly and approachable, he rose through the ranks and couldn't resist when asked to nominate for federal parliament. With a previous name change to Ern Rickard, he'd taken Australian citizenship and nominated, campaigning for the federal seat of Mainwaring in 1975, the year Labor prime minister Gough Whitlam was dismissed.

'Go, Ernie! Go, Ernie!'

The locals were firmly behind him and, running against the anti-Labor tide, Ern Rickard was successful in the subsequent election in December 1975. Could you believe it? Federal member for Mainwaring, yet all the time a Stasi plant.

'Comrade Neumann, I call you to duty!'

Walter Neumann was the next chosen. Dreschner had spoken.

'Sir, I am at your disposal and ready to serve the cause!'

Once again, Neumann had gone through the same modus operandi. Forest camp and language training. A spiriting into West Germany and false residency there. Application to migrate to Australia in 1970, where he acquired citizenship in the minimum time, followed by union membership. Here a variation: Walter Neumann, with a name change to Wal Newell, would play his part as a union leader rather than member of parliament. But it would be just as essential to their assured ultimate success. Establishing himself in a regional New South Wales location, Wal Newell became head of the powerful Union of Allied Rural Industries. A political force whose time would surely come.

Step two for the Ringmaster was to liaise with both of these moles, using his master's research thesis as a cover. With a large amount of Stasi funds transferred to his bank account, money would be no object.

A strange thought for a committed communist.

CHAPTER SEVEN

In all these machinations, the East German Embassy in Canberra was playing an integral part. In no way did the various characters, especially Klaus Ziegler, have to operate without support. Many of the staff were openly members of Otto Dreschner's foreign espionage ministry and delegated to provide assistance as and when it would be needed.

Once alerted Operation Southern Cross was now launched, each was ready to play his part. Though discreetly, lest their host nation's security agency, the Australian Security Intelligence Organisation – ASIO – get wind of their plans. Even arousing local police suspicions was a definite no-no.

With the chancery located in Beagle Street, Red Hill and the residence in Pridham Street, Farrer, the embassy was a formidable establishment. Agents such as Ziegler could access either building but preferably the residence, which had secret meeting rooms included. These were regularly swept for listening devices, as nobody could be sure what ASIO was up to.

For its part, Australia under the Whitlam government had established diplomatic relations with the German Democratic Republic the very month it came to power in December 1972. Its official building in East Berlin had been completed in 1975, just before Whitlam lost office. Otto Dreschner had ensured a large number of listening devices were secreted in both the roof spaces and walls, since then regularly monitored. There was nothing from that interception to indicate Operation Southern Cross would be compromised. Nor, fortunately, any perceived threat at all to Code 1990 meeting the astrologer's target.

'Comrade Ziegler, a toast to your coming success! I realise it will be some years until it's finally accomplished, but nevertheless, I salute you! I've been fully apprised by East Berlin.'

The ambassador was lavish in his praise. He, too, was looking forward to putting one over the much-hated capitalist system and gaining a considerable personal reward.

Klaus Ziegler's clandestine visit to the residence in Farrer gave him every cause for optimism. So far, every step since his arrival had been achieved seamlessly. However, there was still plenty on the to-do list.

Next, one big step in his secret mission.

No doubt a long road ahead.

With a little while until he was required to attend the university bridging course, the so-called private overseas student needed to fit in a trip to Western Australia to check the state of play with Ern Rickard. Called Ernie by the locals? A peculiar country, that was for sure.

Ziegler marvelled at the desert continent below him as his Trans Australia Airlines flight spanned the huge distance between the eastern and western state capitals. It seemingly went on forever. Now their destination was approaching at last, and he refastened his seatbelt. The pilot began the descent. The aircraft was being buffeted by the forces of nature, but they were coming in. Not long now. Almost down. *Boomp!* The crosswind resulted in a slightly bumpy landing at Perth Airport, that being the only glitch he perceived.

'Welcome to Western Australia!' the cheery flight attendant greeted him as he departed the aircraft.

'Thanks.' His reply was offhanded and distracted as he looked towards the terminal and his welcomer.

Rickard was there to meet him, and they hugged as though old friends, despite having never previously met. Each had been thoroughly briefed by the Stasi, so, after the pleasantries, they cut to the chase. It was great for both to be able to speak German again. Driving back from the airport, Rickard suggested a detour via Kings Park. They could walk around and say whatever they wanted in the open air to allay any fear of eavesdroppers. Who knew who could understand German? Ziegler agreed.

It was a magnificent open area, apparently extending for a vast distance. A terrific boon for any city and a great Perth feature. How did these capitalists, these exploiters of workers, manage it? Ziegler would have to learn. For now, it was back to the task at hand, and he had an immediate question. 'Will there be sufficient support for what we plan to do when the time is right? I realise you need what is called here "electorate backing", something quite unknown at home.'

'Yes, comrade. I don't doubt it.'

'You'll need to brief me on the rules for the Australian Labor Party meeting detailed in my official papers and exactly what action you intend to take.'

Rickard filled him in completely.

'Fantastic. And there's no doubt you'll get re-elected?'

'None. I hold Mainwaring by a margin of eighteen percent. Should there be problems, ALP Head Office will intervene. I know Party rules.'

'Magnificent, comrade. Well, I'm impressed by what I've seen so far. I think Mainwaring's going to play a significant part in world history. How about treating me to a grand tour? I've heard your electorate is quite extensive.'

'It is, and I'll do exactly that. But first, fancy a ferry ride to Rottnest Island?'

'Where? Rats?'

Rickard explained, and told him the Dutch explorers gave

the island its name. No, the little creatures found there weren't rats, but cute Australian animals called quokkas. All the tourists loved them. Unique.

An hour later, Ziegler thrilled at the ferry crossing to Perth's famous offshore island.

On arrival, Rickard arranged for them to hire bikes, which they used to circumnavigate the popular tourist destination. Ziegler was mightily impressed. Stopping, they took in the vista from a slight rise, surveying the scene between there and the city in the distance.

Ziegler had a moment of introspection.

'Comrade, when the revolution comes, let's give this place a new name!'

'Such as?'

'Red Island! Why should the capitalist Dutch have all the credit?'

Rickard laughed. 'Consider it done!'

Being alone, they enthusiastically burst into the *Internationale*. It was a stirring moment. Renaming this quaint island would be the least of the changes Australia – and the world – would face. They'd better get used to it.

Plenty to come.

Then Ziegler had one more request for when they got back to Perth.

'Oh, and I want to allay any possible suspicion by being a "dinkum Aussie", as they say. Can you take me to a TAB and fill me in on exactly how you put a bet on a horse?'

'Sure can.'

'I've watched videos on it back home while in training, but nothing beats a real-life experience. I know about betting for a win and a place. Not sure about a quinella. And just what are quaddies? Should I bet with the bookies? Also, please explain a daily double.'

'No worries, mate. She's apples!'

'What? Please explain!'

Ern Rickard was pleased to do just that. Klaus Ziegler had much to consider when he eventually flew back east, and it wasn't all about espionage.

An account with a local bookie would be just the ticket.

CHAPTER EIGHT

One aspect of Klaus Ziegler's brief was to research the various US bases in Australia. An integral part of the overall Stasi aim for world domination was neutralising their effect. Once his political science bridging course was complete, and just before commencing his master's degree proper, Ziegler gave some thought to this task.

'OK, let's look at North West Cape first,' went his self-talk as he opened the file obtained from his embassy.

Now named the Naval Communication Station Harold E. Holt, it was built in 1967 after approval from the federal government. Considered a joint US-Australian defence facility, the base was located just north of the town of Exmouth, Western Australia. That town had been built at the same time as the station to both provide support for it and house the various families of the American personnel involved. Its name honoured former Australian prime minister Harold Holt, who disappeared while swimming and presumably drowned. Holt's body was never recovered.

A glance at the map showed the communication station was situated in one of the remoter areas of that vast state. Surely anyone visiting the area would come under immediate suspicion? A risk he wasn't yet prepared to take.

The file revealed it was an important linchpin in the overall US defence strategy, providing radio communication with American and Australian ships and submarines in both the Pacific and Indian Oceans. There were multiple tall radio towers, which were visible for a vast distance.

'A hard nut to crack for now. I understand what they mean by the tyranny of distance.' Nevertheless, he made a mental note to follow it up when the opportunity presented itself.

Ziegler then considered another possibility: Pine Gap in the Northern Territory.

While even remoter, in fact, than North West Cape, Pine Gap had the advantage of being based only a few kilometres away from the Central Australian town of Alice Springs. 'The Alice', as many called it, was a popular tourist mecca, a visit to which would be quite normal.

So what did the file on Pine Gap reveal?

The latest early 1984 update called it a Joint Defence Space Research Facility, operated in this way by Australia and its American ally. Yes, the hated US Central Intelligence Agency, the CIA, had their grubby fingers in it! Oh, the location was cleverly chosen, right in the centre of this vast continent. Too far away from Soviet submarines in international waters to be able to intercept radio signals.

'Curse the US and their lackeys!' Ziegler spat out, before controlling himself.

Pine Gap, he then read, monitored American spy satellites as they passed over a significant part of the globe. And it did more, much more than that. While officially undertaking 'space research', Pine Gap gave first warning of ballistic missile launches and thus was an integral part of the American defence strategy.

Ziegler made a personal resolution to do what he could to neutralise the hated base.

'*Himmel*, I'd better get moving!' he decided. 'I've got a window of opportunity before the academic year starts.'

He'd already gone through the university enrolment process, and all was ready for his commencement. He'd only have to attend in person periodically, as he'd elected to do his master's by thesis rather than scheduled class attendance. Such flexibility suited him just fine.

Visiting his local travel agent, Glebe Getaways, he booked his flight to Alice Springs with an open-dated return as well as accommodation right in town. He used an alias for security.

'Enjoy the Red Centre!' the happy travel agent wished him. 'First trip there?'

'Yes, I'm looking forward to a memorable experience. A trip to look back on,' he replied meaningfully. *More than you expect, honey!* went his train of thought as he collected his tickets and left with a brief goodbye.

She'd never know. For Klaus Ziegler, it was not a tourist trip, but a mission.

CHAPTER NINE

Trans Australia Airlines arranged a flight that was equally as pleasant as his previous one to Western Australia, with a trouble-free landing at Alice Springs Airport that was a few minutes ahead of schedule. Pleasantly farewelled, as before, from the aircraft by the supervising flight attendant, with the rest of the crew nodding their approval, he entered the terminal.

A delay in luggage collection from the carousel annoyed him, but he put this inconvenience to one side. He made up for this by being fortunate enough to catch a taxi into town immediately.

On the drive, he admired the beauty of the Central Australian desert surrounding him, its redness broken by as much greenery as the town could provide. Different from Germany!

Once settled in his motel room, Ziegler reflected on his next move.

Getting to know the locality was always his primary aim. So he took a walk and within a short time booked an orientation trip around Alice Springs with Town Tours. The van he shared with a handful of other tourists was basic but adequate, with commentary provided by an obliging driver.

At the end, he collected a map of the region plus various publicity pamphlets. The system lacked the Germanic precision he was used to, but when in Rome...

While Pine Gap base itself wasn't actually marked on the map, probably for security reasons, he knew where it was located. Exactly eighteen kilometres south-west of the town. So how to access it? Like any other espionage agent, he knew to watch for opportunities. One always crops up. First step, analyse how the facility worked and what the staff did.

'Where's that briefing paper?' Ziegler asked himself. Finding it, he absorbed the facts. There were about four hundred personnel in the workforce. In the operational area, there were three sections: Satellite Station Keeping, Signals Processing and Signals Analysis.

Interesting. He read on.

Staff were issued a colour-coded pass and normally limited to their own section. Mostly, they lived in town and were transported to and from the base each workday by a series of buses. Identification passes were checked before they were admitted to their work area.

So how could security be breached? Once again, look for chances.

Reading further, there was a reasonable amount of personnel rotation. While many of the Americans were married with families, a significant number were single and appointed for a precise project then rotated out.

Single men, probably new to town, presented a definite opportunity.

'What did the van driver say?' Ziegler asked himself.

His espionage training had taught him to absorb every item of information he came across and be alert to every conversation. People often reveal precious nuggets of intelligence in casual talk. And van drivers, with an eager audience of tourists, love to talk. He quickly remembered...

'Yair, you lot. See the pub on our left? The Desert Sands? The Yanks working out at Pine Gap love to drink there. The publican plays right up to them with a big American flag hanging over the bar. He has prize giveaways on important US holidays such as the Fourth of July and Thanksgiving. They feel right at home, those from desert states like Arizona and New Mexico especially. They love spending their bucks there, let me tell you! A smart man, that Bob McGill, the publican!'

'Thanks, driver. Perhaps I should have given you a bigger tip!'

The 'tourist' gave himself an imaginary high-five.

By seven o'clock that evening, he was treating himself to a pub dinner in the Desert Sands and carefully watching the American servicemen beginning to arrive and order drinks. Wanting to keep himself as alert as possible, his drink of choice was a Claytons. So he kept observing...

His dinner finished and another Claytons in front of him, Ziegler noticed a young American in uniform come in hesitantly. This man was alone. Clean-shaven with a very short haircut, aged twenty-five or so, he certainly seemed unsure of himself. He had no identification tag but must have been one of the base personnel. Ziegler was going to chance his luck.

'G'day, mate!' he opened, putting on his best Australian accent, a tactic he'd been perfecting since his arrival. 'You look a bit lost. Wanna drink?'

'Sure, buddy! I'm new in town, and you're the first person to welcome me. They tell me the custom is to buy someone a "shout" – whatever that is – and then you do the same. Is that right?'

'You're spot on! What's your pleasure? First shout's on me!'

It was a large glass of NT Draught lager, which the American was pleased to sample before returning the favour. Ziegler kept to Claytons. The serviceman hardly noticed.

Pumping him for information, Ziegler introduced himself, giving an alias. The twenty-five-year-old was Rodney Barrett from Arkansas, and he had a six-month posting, as part of his military service, to 'the base' outside Alice Springs. As the evening went on, alcohol loosened his tongue, and he revealed more than was prudent. Far more. Ziegler noted every fact, every one of his senses alive to absorb the illicit information so freely offered.

The mental catalogue was as follows.

The American was posted to Signals Analysis, having studied this field during training at the Pentagon, and was to begin his work tomorrow, after just arriving in Alice Springs that day. He was staying at the Lazy Dreams Motel in a nearby street for a week until he could arrange more long-term accommodation. Then detail after detail of what Signals Analysis entailed, every item recorded mentally.

Stasi training was nothing if not thorough!

'But you'd need a password to access the system, wouldn't you?' Ziegler prodded.

'Yesh, of course,' Rodney replied, well intoxicated. 'But I can't tell you!'

The German's heart sank briefly.

'I thought we were friends!' was the wheedling reply.

'Oh, all right. It's "Clinton". Named after an important guy in our state. I reckon he'll go far, y'all know...'

Ziegler now had all he needed. Time to go.

Buying Rodney a last drink of Draught lager for the night, his final act was to strike once the young man needed another visit to the toilet. As he absented himself and staggered off, Ziegler took out of his pocket a plastic bag of a particular substance and, with nobody looking, all other patrons occupied with their own drinking, tipped it into the young American's newly arrived beer.

'Thanks, Ambassador!' the ruthless espionage agent quietly said to himself. There was no limit to what you could smuggle into the country in a diplomatic pouch, and Ziegler had been supplied with a good quantity in his last secret visit to the GDR embassy's Canberra residence. In this case, GHB, a drug that would put the young resident of Arkansas into a state of unconsciousness for quite a while.

Minutes after Rodney had downed his beer, he was very much the worse for wear. Ziegler helped him back the short distance to the Lazy Dreams, retrieved Rodney's room key from his pocket, opened the door, then carefully let the now-unconscious American sprawl face up on the bed. Ziegler's only compassionate act was to take Rodney's shoes off. Although that was chiefly to ensure a longer and more comfortable sleep.

'So where's his pass?' Ziegler wondered.

The answer was in the motel room's basic wardrobe. There was a brand-spanking-new uniform, hanging up, complete with an identification label attached. All ready for his first day of work tomorrow! Ziegler did a quick check. He was trim enough to fit Rodney's uniform, as the young man was slightly on the well-built side. Close enough to pass, anyway.

Rummaging around for papers, he found them in the bedside drawer. Apart from a very useful bio on Rodney, they gave the details and exact location of the bus pickup for transport to the base. Be there at 0800 sharp!

The only glitch for the photo identification was Rodney's hair colour. Otherwise, their appearances were alike enough for anything other than a quick check. Rodney was dark, whereas Ziegler was fair.

Once again, the magnificent ambassador had foreseen just such a situation. He'd supplied, along with the GHB, tubes of various hair dye. All Ziegler had to do was set the alarm for an early start, dye his hair and be at the bus stop by 0800. A gambler at heart, he would rely on only a cursory identification check if he was with a large group on the bus.

A cinch.

Finding a holdall for the new uniform he'd use, Klaus Ziegler bundled it in, then quietly closed the motel door behind him, putting up the 'Do Not Disturb' sign.

'Pleasant dreams, Rodney!'

With any luck, he'd sleep all day tomorrow and then, his memory wiped clean by the disabling drug, forget everything.

With any luck.

CHAPTER TEN

Klaus Ziegler passed a somewhat restless night, going over the steps he'd take the next day. Waking early, he showered, then applied the hair dye. Great! His breakfast was delivered to his doorstep and quickly devoured. He dressed in Rodney's uniform, grateful the solidly built young man's clothes allowed ample room for him. But not enough to arouse suspicion. Ziegler noted the chevron on each sleeve. Rodney was a private first class, also confirmed by his official papers.

'Show time!' he exclaimed to nobody, then locked his room and walked the distance to the bus stop.

Always early, as he approached, he noticed other Americans making their way over. He slowed his pace, not wanting to have to engage in unnecessary conversation. He needn't have worried.

'How's it going, buddy?'

He heard that more than once from those around him. The animated banter between the many well-acquainted Americans was a welcome distraction. As a newcomer, he was largely ignored but made it his business to smile and nod if anyone caught his eye. With the bus arriving right on 0800, he showed his pass to the driver, who motioned to him to find a seat. A window seat suited him fine, allowing him to look away into the distance.

'Can I join you, soldier?' A polite enquiry from an African-American private who needed a place. He seemed less than fully alert.

'Sure, buddy, sure. Take a seat.'

Ziegler used his best Southern accent, something perfected in the forest training camp, just in case it would be needed. They were big on language and accents training.

'Where ya from?' his fellow passenger opened.

'Little Rock, Arkansas. And you?'

'Phoenix, Arizona. Ever been there? It's a great state, ya know. Plenty of wide-open spaces.'

'Can't say I have. Do you like desert life? I guess it's got its pluses.'

'Sure do, and yer right. I love Phoenix. And for my part, I've never been to Little Rock...'

With that, the still-tired Arizonan seemed to doze off, suiting Ziegler well. The less conversation, the better.

With no competing traffic, the bus soon arrived at the base entrance, stopping for security. Two burly military police boarded and greeted the driver, then glanced at those on board. Ziegler felt his hair stand on end. With nothing suspicious noted, they left with a cursory 'Drive on.'

Once the boom gate lifted, the bus did. It stopped in front of the main building, and the passengers began to alight.

So where was his section?

As they all filed past security, showing their identification, Ziegler fell in with those displaying passes of a similar colour. Good tactic – they led him straight to his work area.

Those who already had assignments went straight to their workstations. Knowing he was a newbie, Ziegler found an officer and saluted, announcing himself.

'Private First Class Barrett reporting for duty, sir!' He offered his papers, which the officer perused then handed back to him.

'Glad you're here, Barrett. Plenty for you to do in Signals Analysis. Hope you enjoy your six-month posting. I'll get PFC Di Claudio to give you some background and get you up to speed. You'll attend an official orientation program later, but we're short-staffed at the moment, so it'll have to wait.'

'That's fine, thank you, sir.'

So he spent a valuable hour being instructed by PFC Di Claudio on the intricacies of signals analysis. With permission, he was able to make notes on a pocket-sized notepad to 'assist his orientation', as he put it. Di Claudio was quite obliging. Ziegler noticed there were a few Australian staff, but most were American, and he asked about that.

'Yep, we've only allowed the Aussies to come into the section in the last four years. Prior to that, they were banned.'

'Really? In their own country?'

''Fraid so! That's security for you.'

'Well, you can't be too careful!'

Never was a truer word spoken.

After the first hour, Ziegler was given the task of monitoring signals that came through from American anti-missile and anti-aircraft radars. By so doing, he was able to find their locations in various parts of the world, highly useful from an espionage point of view. He noticed there were a number in the border areas west of the GDR, with the rest established in places, such as Turkey, bordering the Soviet Union.

All of this went into his small notebook, with their various codenames.

After that, he moved to signals coming from American submarines on duty in both the Indian and Pacific Oceans. Then the different signals from Russian subs. He was given a chart with the code signs of their NATO allies, plus Australian subs. Pine Gap was a treasure trove of information! Everything useful went into the notebook, although he had to be careful not to arouse suspicion. A friendly wave or nod according to office etiquette seemed to allay any suspicions.

'Coffee break!' Di Claudio announced, and the two had a friendly chat over a cuppa. The PFC was a native of upstate New York, it turned out. Ziegler was glad he had no detailed knowledge of Arkansas.

Minutes before lunch, Ziegler had just finished analysing the details of telephone calls members of the Kremlin had been making to their far-flung armed forces when his sixth sense told him something was up.

The atmosphere had changed.

Nonchalantly sidling over to the window, he saw a Northern Territory police car below, with two constables animatedly discussing something with the base security MPs. They were looking around, obviously eager to follow up on some mission.

He had to take action.

Not even bothering to collect his stolen identification papers, Ziegler surreptitiously left the Signals workstation and made his way down to the back of the building. Adrenaline pumping, he needed an opportunity for a quick exit.

What luck! A laundry van, from 'Alice Springs Cleaning', its back doors open, was parked right there. With a number of bags already inside, the driver must be collecting a final load before going back to town.

In Ziegler jumped, pulling the bags of dirty washing on top of him, then lay as quietly as possible, his heart pumping fit to burst. Would his luck hold?

It did.

Seconds later, the driver threw a final bag on top of the others, slammed the doors shut then started the van, motoring towards the base security gate. The driver slowed as he approached.

Would the guards do a check?

Right at that moment, another police car arrived, urgently trying to gain entry. With it taking the guards' attention, they simply waved to the driver to go straight through, lifting the boom gate to allow his easy exit. The police remonstrated with the guards until allowed entry, then sped in the direction of the main building. What a furore.

So far, so good. Against the odds, Klaus Ziegler had escaped.

CHAPTER ELEVEN

With the immediate crisis over, the East German spy did a quick calculation. He hadn't given the hapless American soldier enough of the drug to keep him quiet for the day. Barrett must have woken up earlier than expected and raised the alarm. He would sure have some explaining to do, but that was no longer Ziegler's concern.

Yes, his heart still racing, he realised there was one desperate way he could make his complete escape from the area, as the police would be on the lookout at the airport.

First step, a clean break from the van when back in the Alice. Top priority. Looking around, there was a little room left inside, and he hoped there'd be another stop in town.

There was.

With the doors opened for the last collection and the driver briefly out of sight, Ziegler jumped straight out of the van and moved away briskly, recognising roughly where he was. The next step in his plan was to get out of his conspicuous American uniform, back into his normal clothes.

Finding his motel, he was fortunate enough to unlock his room door without being noticed. Washing out his hair dye and changing back into his own clothes, Ziegler gathered his pack, called at the office to pay his bill, then walked away as fast as he could without arousing suspicion.

Next stop, the main highway.

Approaching it, he enjoyed more luck than he deserved. Right in front of him was the depot for Centralia Transports, with a huge semitrailer idling away, ready to depart. He didn't care in which direction. The driver, Digger Jackson, was having a quick cigarette before setting off. Ziegler got his attention and used his best French accent.

'My friend, any chance of ze lift to where you're going? I'm hitching around Australia.'

'Darwin suit ya? I'm leavin' in two minutes, after I finish me gasper. Could stand some company. A lonely job, ya know.'

'Perfect. You can tell me about Australia. Many thanks.'

So 'Gustave Lenoir' jumped aboard, throwing his bag in the space behind the passenger's seat, settled back and listened to a monologue on the history and people of Australia, most of which he knew already. What a character was 'the Digger'. An old army man who'd moved to his present employment. Could talk for hours and did so. A lifesaver for now, but Ziegler would have liked an off switch.

Heading north, there was a comfort stop in Tennant Creek, then Digger drove through the night to Darwin. As dawn broke, there was Centralia's Darwin depot right ahead.

'So, Gus, where do ya want to get off?'

'Right here is fine, thanks. Is zat ze road into ze city?'

'Sure is, just a klick or two at the most.'

'Zat's fine. Thanks for ze lift. Good luck, Digger.'

'You too. See ya!'

You meet all types in the Centre, Digger thought.

After a stop at a café for breakfast, Ziegler caught a taxi to the airport, where he bought a ticket for the first available flight to Sydney, using yet another assumed name. The flight departed three hours later, a nervous wait in case the local police got onto him.

They didn't.

It would be quite some time before the Alice Springs police

got the full story from PFC Rodney Barrett, joined the various dots, gave up on a search of the airport, questioned semitrailer drivers about likely hitchhikers leaving town, then tracked down Digger Jackson.

'Well, stone the crows! Knock me down with a feather. Some sorta spy? I was lucky he didn't hijack me rig!'

'Not his MO, apparently, but you had a lucky escape.'

The police left the file open for further action.

Once safely back in Glebe, the daring agent rested for a day then set off on the drive to Canberra. The East German ambassador would be on the edge of his chair digesting all the information from Ziegler's notebook jottings. He'd give the ambassador chapter and verse and put in a full report. Pine Gap was a treasure trove for the GDR.

Definitely one in the eye for the hated capitalists.

CHAPTER TWELVE

Four weeks later, there was much excitement in the Kremlin, Moscow as Soviet General Secretary Konstantin Chernenko called a special meeting of the chiefs of the three armed forces. While those of the army and air force were certainly needed, the main thrust of the meeting was an upgrading of naval strength.

The navy was paramount. The admiral of the fleet, Vladimir Rostov, had lobbied hard for this meeting and, as his position justified, had pride of place in the front row. He hoped Chernenko would take a hard-line position after he heard what Rostov would outline.

With the chairman first acknowledging Chernenko, who'd just begun his tenure as general secretary, he called upon the admiral to address the meeting.

A supremely confident Admiral Rostov took the floor.

'Comrades, thank you for your attendance. I am apprised by our Committee for State Security – the KGB – that there have been significant developments away from Europe, which, as you know, has so far been the focus of our concerns. If we are to outflank the West and win the Cold War, it is essential to strike where least expected. Our loyal allies in the German Democratic Republic have prepared an operation in just such a place, and my information has been relayed by their Security Ministry, the

Stasi. I regret the actual details must for now remain top secret for obvious reasons, but in time, all will of course be revealed.'

Everyone nodded. The reputation of the Stasi was well-known.

'The Stasi has a well-prepared plan to turn the tide against the West in the coming years. They have a multi-pronged project. We need to be in lockstep with them and poised to take action at the right time.'

Konstantin Chernenko jumped to his feet. 'Admiral Rostov, how does this square with our stated policy of general liberalisation? I urge us to continue with that course!'

Rostov continued. 'Of course, Comrade Chernenko, it's a fair question. We continue with that policy, naturally. We'll invite foreign leaders to Moscow to discuss trade, foreign policy and the like. But all the time, our stated intention is to prevail. By becoming world masters, we'll put our own stamp on liberalisation!' Oh, yes, he'd do it his way, by hook or by crook.

Chernenko pulled a face. This wasn't how he saw it.

Rostov added, 'Getting us into the right position to be world masters will involve a significant financial outlay. I propose a five-year plan. If the general secretary approves the required expenditure, the fleets will be ready to play their part!'

Well, how could Chernenko object? The Pacific Fleet would be backed up by the Northern, Black Sea and Baltic Fleets, in addition to other elements.

By his reading of the room, Rostov was convinced he had the meeting in the palm of his hand.

'We're at a critical juncture. In particular, it's essential for the Pacific Fleet to be built up, with the port of Vladivostok modernised to take increased traffic. As I've just outlined, we have five years at most! I want that fleet size trebled and Vladivostok turned into a military and naval hub as never before. We will also use the adjacent Kuril Islands to house the expanded fleet. I propose one hundred billion roubles be allocated for the task and table this budget paper by way of explanation.'

A great coup to use those former Japanese islands – they were highly strategic.

With the clamour of general approval, Konstantin Chernenko realised he'd been rolled. All he could do was make the best of it. This wasn't how he saw 'general liberalisation'. One hundred billion roubles! He'd risk bankrupting the Soviet Union!

Rostov continued, more reasonably. 'General Secretary, our new aircraft carrier, the *Tbilisi*, will lead the way on this. Rest assured, I'll take special care with the build-up.'

'I expect nothing less, Admiral Rostov.'

'And may I outline my plan of action for when all this is accomplished, esteemed comrade?'

Rostov was insistent. He knew where he was going. In any case, he had inside knowledge Chernenko wouldn't be in the position of general secretary for more than a few months at best, given his state of health. Then Rostov would be in the box seat to influence his likely successor.

Chernenko nodded.

'Firstly, note this. I want our five-year construction project to actually be done in three! Yes, we'll work the shipyards round the clock, if necessary, and I'll supervise. Make no mistake, I'll crack the whip! Then, as naval chief, I intend to take on the US fleet in the Western Pacific. Force them back to Hawaii. I want our navy, army and air force to dominate as far south as New Zealand.

That's how the Soviet Union will win the Cold War!'

They rose as one to give Vladimir Rostov and a very reluctant Konstantin Chernenko a standing ovation. The latter would have to sit down with his treasurer to scratch around and find the huge number of roubles needed – no easy task.

Did Rostov care? Not a bit.

After that, the vodka flowed freely to celebrate. Just as well the secretaries recorded all the salient points. They knew what would come next.

Not one armed forces chief was in a fit state to work for the rest of the day.

Especially Admiral Rostov.

CHAPTER THIRTEEN

Having settled into Sydney by purchasing a home in the same suburb, Kensington, where they had first found a flat, the Schneiders embraced their new life with gusto. Jonas enjoyed his lecturing role at the university and published a number of papers. Ursula initially found a position as a kindergarten teacher but soon turned to her real love, writing children's books.

Local readers lapped them up. *Great Gertie Goanna, Elusive Edrick Echidna* and other books featuring kangaroos, galahs, wombats and possums became well-known. There was also a beautiful one based on the adventures of a flock of budgerigars.

'Bluey and Goldie chirped to each other that summer's day high in the ghost gum...'

By the 1980s, she was invited onto children's television programs and undertook book launches not only in Sydney suburbs but in various regional towns. Her method was to contact local libraries and organise a talk, with samples of her books for sale. Librarians would ensure publicity and plenty of interest. If possible, Ursula organised a circuit, going from one town to the other before returning to Sydney.

In this way, she became an acclaimed author. Hundreds of kids knew of the wonderful exploits of Gertie and Edrick. Not to mention Bluey and Goldie!

In mid-1985, while on a country promotional tour, she left the local town library carrying a pile of books. Perhaps too many. As she came out onto the footpath, she collided with a man walking past, and the books went flying. New books, so quite precious!

'I'm so sorry, I didn't notice you!' He was evidently somewhat distraught. A gentleman, he not only helped her pick up the books but offered to carry them to her car a short distance away. She gratefully agreed.

'It was really my fault – I wasn't watching.'

Ursula had indeed been a little distracted. Fortunately, there was little, if any, damage to the books, as they'd been carefully wrapped.

'Thank you again.'

'No problem. I was happy to help.' His gaze met hers.

Evidently, he had business in the same street, as she noticed he checked his watch before hurrying off. She hoped her misadventure hadn't delayed him. *It's always heartening,* she thought, *when people put themselves out to help someone, even after such a minor incident. It certainly reinforces your faith in human nature. A genuine good Samaritan.*

Had the man read her thoughts, he would have smiled. He'd never been called that in his life. The term wasn't in his playbook.

As for Ursula Schneider, she consoled herself by concluding her visit had been successful, with many books sold, despite her having to return a bundle to her car. She'd learned a lot about the history of this popular scenic town, who had founded it and when, thanks to a briefing by Tahlia Grace, the informative librarian. Very interesting...

Well, where to next? Perhaps a cup of coffee in a local café before her next port of call? She'd declined Tahlia's kind offer of refreshment, preferring to concentrate on her presentation. But now would be a good opportunity.

A double cappuccino would hit the spot. Then she'd head off towards Sydney. One more appointment, this time in another beautiful tourist location. Yes, she loved learning as much as possible about her new country. It gave her all the more fodder for her books. *Great Gertie Goanna* would keep climbing trees for years to come.

After downing her cappuccino, she realised she'd better get going. No doubt more helpful librarians, eager children and delighted parents would be waiting.

That accomplished, it'd be home sweet home.

CHAPTER FOURTEEN

In his busy life criss-crossing the continent to liaise with Ern Rickard about getting government MPs onside, connecting with Wal Newell to ensure unions' cooperation, then doing the minimum for his master's degree studies, there was one factor Klaus Ziegler didn't foresee.

Romance.

Fellow student Xanthe Young was impressed by this handsome man from West Germany, that being his cover story.

Xanthe and family were originally from Mudgee, north-west of Sydney, but had lived in a spacious home in Barker Road, Strathfield for some years. She, too, was enrolled in her master's degree but was undertaking it by coursework. She was slightly envious of her classmate, who had a travelling brief and spent only a short time in class, conferring with his supervisor.

Twenty-three years of age and highly intelligent, with attractive, long dark hair, she definitely caught Ziegler's eye. The two spent many an afternoon in cafés discussing both their course and the numerous interests they appeared to have in common. Yet she kept mentioning his frequent absences and seemed concerned his studies could be affected.

'Xanthe, my thesis requires me to travel and do a lot of interviews.'

'Yes, but I've heard Dr Wexall isn't too pleased... he wants more progress.'

In fact, so demanding were Ziegler's visits and espionage plans that he failed to make even the slightest course progress, resulting in a warning from his supervisor, Dr Felix Wexall. As the system demanded, this fact was relayed through to the Department of Immigration's Kendrick Findlay, who called him in for a progress consultation. An unneeded complication, as his visa depended on academic effort. He knew the department had a system of warnings to be issued to dilatory students.

'Herr Ziegler,' Findlay began, liking any opportunity to show off his German, 'I must ask you to give more attention to your studies so you achieve your degree in the requisite time. I trust your tertiary supervisor won't have to contact us again. I would hate to have to issue an official warning.'

'Rest assured, Mr Findlay, I'll meet the course requirements from now on and put in the time to complete my thesis.'

Yes, he had a plan to do just that.

'Thanks, Herr Ziegler. I look forward to it.'

As he left, Klaus Ziegler knew exactly what to do. The good old embassy would have the answer. There was one clerk in particular, a political expert, who would provide what he needed. He'd bowl it up to Felix Wexall well and truly. Xanthe could then stop nagging... er, advising him.

The embassy never failed to come through when needed. There was nobody more politically experienced and aware than an East German, and the designated clerk, Rudolf Wohl, was now rostered to undertake the task of completing the master's thesis. What was a little plagiarism when the future of the GDR was at stake? A mere peccadillo.

By the end of 1985, the thesis was duly finished and handed to

Dr Wexall, receiving a High Distinction. Xanthe gave Ziegler a congratulatory kiss.

At the start of the following year, he began his Doctor of Philosophy studies, selecting the title *The Art of Politics in a Post-Political Age*. Curious.

The embassy clerk began his research.

Ziegler's meetings with Ern Rickard and Wal Newell revolved around the big step in Operation Southern Cross, a planned coup, with the date circled. They weren't going to rush it – rather, they'd gather their 'evidence' carefully. But the timing was critical.

It had to be utterly convincing.

Xanthe's parents were more than keen to meet their daughter's new beau, who spent many an evening regaling them with his 'life' in West Germany, using an appropriate cover story. They appeared to be very impressed. Did they see a marriage on the horizon?

Politically, the next hurdle was the 1987 election. Hawke had to be re-elected. Every effort was made to ensure this. All would be lost if the Coalition came back into office. Essential, too, for Ern Rickard to hold his seat. Eighteen percent was a big enough buffer. Or so they hoped.

For now, roll on 1986.

CHAPTER FIFTEEN

She was in a rush that afternoon following an essential business meeting on a day when many were too distracted to work efficiently. She was uninterested in lunch parties or dress-ups in weird costumes. Not for her, the crazy hats or fascinators many women delighted in. No, she was focussed on her next enterprise. Such was her upbringing. Her loving husband was of a similar disposition, although he was at his usual workplace and absorbed with his own projects.

A delightful spring day with a cloudless sky, deep cerulean. *Goodness me,* she thought, *that meeting went well.* 'My next production will be a beauty! Now, I'll dash across the road here. Hardly a car in sight!'

In her haste, she failed to look. A fatal mistake.

As for the driver of a certain Ford Falcon, his totally different business meeting, a phone conference called urgently by two dedicated partners, had delayed his preferred indulgence in a habit he'd developed about three years ago. As one of the callers was overseas, he completely ignored the importance of today in Australia. Nevertheless, the man had the opportunity to make a considerable financial outlay.

As he sped along in his Ford Falcon sedan, rather too fast, he realised the time!

'It's almost on!' Fiddling with his radio dial, he looked down to ensure his tuning was exact. 'Blow it, what's up with the radio?'

He didn't want to miss a second of the broadcast. Only in the last second did he look up again. Too late!

Thump!

The distracted woman stepped right into his path as she crossed Alison Road, Randwick and was flung metres into the air, landing awkwardly then rolling into the gutter. She lay quite motionless.

He skidded to a halt, panic-stricken.

In his fright, he didn't even hear the progress of the Melbourne Cup race run that Tuesday, 4 November 1986. Nor, two minutes later, At Talaq's stunning win. The man had bet on Rising Fear for both a win and a place. It would be a small compensation that the horse had come in second.

Such matters, previously so attention-grabbing, were now completely unimportant in the light of the crisis now facing Klaus Ziegler. Shocked, he looked around. With almost everyone concentrating on the race, an Australian tradition, there was no traffic. He dashed over to the woman lying face up in the gutter, blood trickling from the terrible impact.

As he looked right into her eyes, she showed a flicker of recognition but said nothing.

She looked familiar, and Ziegler racked his brains as to why and where from. No answer came. Self-preservation then kicked in. She was practically done for, so no point in hanging around. His whole mission could be in jeopardy if he called the cops and they did a thorough investigation.

No, better to just disappear.

Seeing there was still no traffic, the ruthless spy ran back to his Ford, gunned the motor and took off along Alison Road, only slowing down when he was safely away from the scene. His vehicle was damaged by the impact, and he'd have to activate an emergency plan to cope.

Once back in Glebe, Ziegler was grateful for the lockup garage at his home, immediately concealing the damaged Ford until he could work out what to do.

'*Donnerwetter*! What a pickle!'

He consoled himself with a large dose of schnapps, hoping the alcoholic remedy might help, before he reached for his phone.

'Hello, Embassy, I have a problem…'

Mere seconds after Ziegler had callously departed the scene, young Sophie van den Bosch, who had just finished a shift as a retail assistant at a suburban children's clothing store, was walking home along that road. She was shocked to come across the dying woman sprawled in the gutter and rushed to help. Putting her own coat under the poor woman's head, Sophie waved to flag down any vehicles for help. Traffic was now returning, and several cars began to stop after her frantic action.

Sophie got right back to the woman, who wanted to say something. Just one word.

'Korff!'

It was as clear as a bell.

She repeated 'Korff!' then her eyes glazed over and her life force ebbed.

Ursula Schneider was dead.

- - -

With his self-preservation meter metaphorically off the charts, Ziegler relied on all the wiles of his embassy in Canberra to get him out of this dilemma. One of the Stasi officers there advised him to wait till it was dark, then take his damaged Ford to a safe house in Yagoona, in Sydney's west. It had an attached car repair workshop. He'd also have a loaner car while the repairs were made but was advised to leave it in his Glebe garage unless absolutely necessary and to transact business either over the phone or by using public transport. It was helpful that in the inner city, people minded their own business and were less nosy. Or cared less.

Despite this, Ziegler was still shaken. An unforeseen tragedy. A pity about that woman – where had he seen her before?

But then he pulled his thoughts back on track. There was an election coming next year, and he had to ensure his co-conspirators were on track for their 1988 plan's climax. This was what had been discussed in the conference call with Otto Dreschner and Ern Rickard. A death was just a speed bump in the road. Treating himself liberally to Jägermeister helped convince him of this.

In the scheme of things, one dead woman hardly mattered.

Simply collateral damage.

\- - -

'Yes, she said Korff! I don't understand it, but it was obviously important!'

Sophie van den Bosch gave Randwick Police a full report, emphasising the dying Ursula's last word. The constables were as puzzled as the teenager but dutifully recorded it. Confirming neither Sophie nor the drivers who stopped to assist had seen the impact, nor had any of the immediate homeowners, the police turned to the accident scene.

A small scraping of paint was obtained from Ursula's body, plus one from the roadway. There was also a minor amount of debris from the vehicle in question. All bagged for analysis.

No driver ever came forward to report their part in the tragedy, and the police did their best to investigate. The lack of witnesses was a real problem. Chemical analysis showed the vehicle was a silver 1982 Ford Falcon, and publicity was given to every repair workshop.

There were no leads. Checking if any such vehicle was disposed of also proved to be a dead end. It was a popular make, and there were too many for an overstretched police force to check effectively, no matter how hard they tried.

Once the Ford was repaired, Ziegler was instructed to drive it to Canberra, where it became an embassy car with diplomatic plates. The ambassador arranged for him to obtain a new Holden instead.

In Glebe, nobody noticed. The anonymity of the inner city.

Ziegler relaxed. The Stasi could do anything. No wonder East Germany would soon rule Europe.

It was a comforting thought.

Jonas Schneider was devastated beyond belief when the police brought the shocking news. Consoled by colleagues and neighbours, once Ursula's funeral was over, he threw himself into research work, detouring from his usual career as an engineer to analyse road trauma. He never gave up on the police finding the person responsible, praying nightly for a favourable outcome. Randwick Police gave him a sympathetic hearing when he visited, outlining every possible scenario.

As time went by, it seemed as though the accident would never be solved. After twelve months, it became a cold case and seemed forgotten. Yet Jonas Schneider remained a man of faith that justice would one day prevail.

'Yes, it'll happen! I feel it in my bones and will never rest till there's an answer. Dear Ursula, I'll love you forever!'

For now, patience would have to remain a virtue.

CHAPTER SIXTEEN

One significant reason for the telling November phone conference call was the intelligence gleaned by the Stasi that Bob Hawke might lose the coming 1987 election. It was essential Labor won, as a Coalition victory would well and truly stymie their plans. An early election in 1984 had reduced Hawke's majority, and should this happen again in 1987, the Coalition would win.

Under no circumstances could this be allowed to occur. Otto Dreschner was insistent.

'Comrade Ziegler, pull out all stops. Hawke must win so he's there in 1988. Rickard must also win and stay there for Mainwaring.'

'Absolutely, Comrade Dreschner.'

That settled it.

The Stasi might have been correct about the ALP's dismal prospects, and Hawke, totally unaware of the cabal being hatched, called the election for July. A double dissolution, with all one hundred and forty-eight seats in the House of Representatives up for election, along with all seventy-six seats in the Senate.

Ziegler and his co-conspirators were on tenterhooks, because for much of the previous three years, the Opposition had led in the polls. During meetings in the embassy, the Stasi had considered extreme means to sabotage the Opposition but aborted these, fearing a sympathetic backlash should an Opposition leader suddenly 'disappear'.

In the end, Opposition disunity did their job for them, and Hawke was able to win a third term. There were drinks all round in the embassy. East Berlin was delighted, and Otto Dreschner gave his astrologer a bonus.

Brunhilde Dreschner didn't know what to think.

'It's a beautiful day, Hazel!' Speaking to his wife, Bob Hawke congratulated himself, quite unaware glasses were being clinked not only in the Canberra embassy but also in East Berlin. Election victory may have been down to Hawke's reformist agenda of floating the Australian dollar, reducing tariffs and reforming the tax system, but machinations behind the scenes played their part. Of the one hundred and forty-eight seats, the government won eighty-six and the Opposition sixty-two. As insurance, the Stasi had put some effort into ensuring seats were won by the Socialist Workers and Communist Parties, but here, they were unsuccessful. Nevertheless, it was a great victory, and all was on track for the climax the following year.

The cheers resounded. To June 1988!

Code 1990 was in sight.

CHAPTER SEVENTEEN

Bill and Maureen Young had their misgivings. They were delighted their only daughter, Xanthe, had a steady boyfriend, one who was obviously intelligent and charming, with what appeared to be a promising academic future. However, they worried about his frequent absences.

'What on earth is he up to, with those travels around Australia?' they quizzed their daughter.

'Oh, don't worry, he has to get background for his thesis. He's going for his PhD, you know.'

Xanthe had gained her master's degree and was now employed by a Liberal member of parliament, doing research. Klaus Ziegler was intensely interested, and Xanthe mistook this for caring about her.

Her parents were no country bumpkins just because they were retired graziers. Having successfully developed a grazing property on Lower Piambong Road, Mudgee, they had sold it for a good price, preferring the more comfortable life in Sydney. However, they definitely missed the wide-open spaces the Mudgee area afforded, comfortable as their Barker Road home was.

They possessed innate intelligence and had a 'feel' about Ziegler. Nothing they could put their finger on – he was just a bit too slick. Not quite enough detail about his family growing up. Where had he learned his impeccable English? His answers were a little too pat. Plausible, certainly, but as Bill Young knew all too well, plausible doesn't necessarily mean true.

So, if he was concealing something, what could it be? Another woman? Financial deceit? Some swindle? Something political? That *was* his line of study.

Talking together, the Youngs listed likely problems. They had used such a tactic when analysing farming problems: drought, flood, plagues of pests such as mice and the like. Country life hadn't been all beer and skittles.

Maureen was a bit more open-minded and tolerant than Bill.

'Let's just watch and wait, Bill. Yes, we've got misgivings, but Xanthe is happy. If something's up, we'll learn more in the course of time.'

'OK, dear, you're right. Watch and wait it is.'

CHAPTER EIGHTEEN

Yesterday had been an extravaganza like no other that she could recall. Millions of Sydneysiders and other fellow Australians had the same memory. The fleet of tall ships entering Sydney Harbour right on cue; the Royal Australian Air Force flyover; Prince Charles's speech; the beaming face of Prime Minister Bob Hawke, exulting in the festivities. Later, night-time fireworks, the sight of which took your breath away, if the ensuing pall of smoke didn't do so on its own.

Absolutely stunning in every way.

How pleased was Detective Sergeant Lillian Boyd her recent promotion had placed her in Sydney at that very moment. That unforgettable day in January 1988, she was just in time to enjoy the festivities celebrating exactly two hundred years' settlement of the wide, brown land. An empathetic woman, Lillian reflected that Aboriginal people had far less reason to be enthusiastic, but hoped there would one day be a means of embracing them more inclusively.

'Welcome to Randwick Police Station, Lillian!'

Inspector Chris O'Rourke was pleased to see his new officer on duty, ready to undertake her first assignment, a matter which had been troubling the station for some time. O'Rourke had forensic science training and approached cases in that way. So far, this one had eluded a solution, and he was determined to find it, if only through Lillian's intervention.

'Thank you, sir. I'm certainly pleased to be here.'

Thirty-six years of age and dedicated to the police force, Lillian had career experience from a number of postings around New South Wales. Originally from the scenic township of Katoomba in the Blue Mountains, she had grown up in a loving family, the younger of two children. Her parents emphasised physical fitness, and many weekends were spent hiking the various tourist tracks. The family operated a business, Summit Books, and once the doors were shut promptly at 12 p.m. each Saturday, it was time to lace on the hiking boots.

Following high school, young Lillian was successful in applying to be a probationary police constable, a calling she pursued with great zeal. After graduation, she excelled in her first placement in Nyngan. Two years later, she met another young constable, who gained her affections. Following eighteen months' courtship, they married. However, with conflict over whether to start a family or focus on their careers, they parted three years afterwards, though amicably. Lillian would have liked a baby, but her husband wasn't so sure. For now, Lillian was devoted to her calling.

'How was Goulburn? I hope you enjoyed it. In any case, you definitely put a dent in the activities of any local crims, according to reports.' O'Rourke seemed impressed by her work record in her recent appointment.

'A great city. The winters were a bit cold for me.'

'Well, you can warm up here and maybe enjoy Coogee Beach on your days off.'

If I get enough time off, Lillian thought. She reckoned there'd be plenty of work to do in Randwick. Chris O'Rourke would demand the highest standards – she'd expect nothing less.

Following introductions and allowing her to settle into her new office, O'Rourke briefed her on her first assignment.

'Lillian, I don't like cold cases, and I realise you're of the same opinion. Your record shows you've already put two to bed. The grazier murder in Canowindra and the mysterious disappearance of that teenage girl in Dubbo.'

'Yes, sir. I'm determined to mark a case closed. I realise how trauma affects families, and a resolution, preferably a conviction of the guilty party, helps them cope.'

'Exactly!' Inspector O'Rourke was delighted they were of the same mind. 'Well, take some time to go through this file.' He placed it squarely in front of her. 'A hit-and-run, more than a year ago. Officially a cold case since last November. Good luck with it.'

Once alone, she turned to the unsolved case of Ursula Schneider's tragic road death. The facts were stark.

Melbourne Cup Day, 1986. Witness statement from Sophie van den Bosch. Nothing available from any other road user or pedestrian witness. Weather report and photos of the scene in Alison Road, with markings by the constables later called to the site. Paint scrapings and report on the make and model of the vehicle concerned. A further report on enquiries at a multitude of car repairers. Photos of poor deceased Ursula.

'Very mysterious!'

Normally, enquiries show up something. Not this time.

She read on.

Next came a heartfelt report from the police interview with Jonas, Ursula's bereaved husband. The poor man was quite inconsolable, but some facts emerged. Ursula was looking forward to finalising another in her series of children's books, with a revised edition of *Great Gertie Goanna*. Her illustrator, who lived on Alison Road, had asked for an urgent meeting to check on progress, with a deadline looming.

'OK, the constables were very thorough. They also interviewed the illustrator, that being Ursula's last known location...'

The cogs kept whirring.

The file showed that the poor woman was unbelievably shocked. She had farewelled Ursula but moved inside immediately after Ursula left. She hadn't heard the impact – it turned out she had thought of watching the horse race on television at the last minute, and the noisy Cup excitement drowned out the outside drama. She only emerged once police vehicles arrived with flashing lights. So there were no actual witnesses.

The best they had to go on was Sophie's statement.

'Korff!' – the dying woman's last word. Then repeated. It obviously meant something.

First step was to interview the two constables who had reported the road death, once Lillian had studied their reports a second time. One was still stationed in Randwick, the other recently transferred to Maroubra. Conveniently close by.

'Great to meet you. Glad you're onto it, Lillian.'

Each was separately grateful. Neither liked loose ends. Or, even worse, justice denied.

However, no leads for now. They had done their job at the time. Though young Sophie had been as helpful as possible, it was sheer bad luck there was no immediate witness. It couldn't have happened at a worse time – the running of the Melbourne Cup – with the normally busy Alison Road almost deserted.

So, a dead end? Not quite.

Lillian studied the known facts. A woman, part of a German migrant couple, a hit-and-run death. It must have been a chance catastrophe. There wasn't the slightest suggestion it was deliberate. She was a harmless children's author, he a respected university lecturer at his workplace at the time. Checked and verified. No, it was definitely an accident. So why didn't the driver stop? Unless he was drunk or drug affected, he would have been cleared of prosecution. Distracted, Ursula must have stepped right in front of him.

'So what was he hiding? And who or what is Korff?'

The check of 1982 Ford Falcon registrations hadn't turned up anyone by that name. Lillian Boyd was now on the hunt.

She'd leave no stone unturned.

CHAPTER NINETEEN

With 1988 well underway, now that the capitalist extravaganza of that year's Australia Day celebrations was yesterday's news, the Stasi conspirators began to finalise their plans for the big coup against Hawke. East Berlin was right behind them, and they had just months for it to climax.

In their different meetings, they had ruminated over what form this political assassination would take. A love triangle or honey trap was considered and had some merit. The Stasi, like the KGB, were very adept at such a lure. However, given the present attitude to the popular prime minister, it could well backfire.

No, it had to be financial. Embezzlement would never wash with the public.

Their file revealed the previous Whitlam Labor government had engineered its own disgrace – unhelped in any way by the machinations of the Stasi – with its infamous Khemlani Loans Affair, where they were completely duped by a wily overseas businessman. How did they fall for it?

So a financial scandal was the answer. They'd fit up something similar on Hawke. Neither he nor his cabinet would see it coming.

Given the time pressure to get it right, Klaus Ziegler had a sudden thought, interrupting their urgent discussions.

'Comrades, I need to get the groundwork right – you can't forget my PhD research. My nuisance of a supervisor has been asking too many questions to which I can't find answers. Yes, I never thought Felix Wexall would throw a spanner in the works every time our mission becomes critical. The man is never satisfied. He keeps pressuring me for more research. So I'll have to clear it with the embassy and get Rudolf there to cough some up, he's practically doing nothing else!'

The embassy clerk was as essential to the mission as anyone else.

Out of necessity, they called a break, allowing Rudolf to be briefed and get to work. If a doctorate was ever to be awarded, it should be in the name of Dr Rudolf. Even so, it was all a complete deception. Smoke and mirrors.

The timing was now decided, for as public an event as was possible. Two of them would be present, the third elsewhere to direct the immediate follow-up. When it worked, it would rock Australia to the core.

The rest of the mission would be like collapsing dominoes.

Hawke to fall. Later – Australia. Then – Cold War victory for the communist powers. Inevitable and glorious.

Workers of the world, unite!

CHAPTER TWENTY

Concentrating hard on the file before her, Lillian Boyd wondered about her next step. There was a heartfelt letter from Jonas Schneider to Inspector O'Rourke pleading for a solution and for the offender to be apprehended and convicted. Time to speak to Mr Schneider. She made the phone call.

His Kensington home was comfortable but definitely lacked a woman's touch. Academic papers were strewn around the lounge room, something the rather fastidious Ursula had discouraged. Each had their own study, he for his research and she for her book writing, but while she was alive, the lounge room was to be kept tidy for visitors. No longer.

'Please come in.'

Jonas seemed eager to have a visitor. Perhaps the widower was quite in need of company. Away from his work environment, he might well feel the pangs of loneliness. There was plenty of support immediately after Ursula's tragic demise, but that had well and truly lessened.

'Mr Schneider, I'll cut to the chase. Your late wife's death has become a cold case. One which I'm determined to solve, if at all possible.'

At that, he brightened considerably.

'Thank you, Detective Sergeant. I really appreciate that news.

I pray every night for a solution and justice.' She noticed an open Bible on a side table and didn't doubt it was true.

'Sure, I feel the same way. Now, I'm intrigued by Ursula's last word, "Korff", and regard it as a clue. So far, it's turned up nothing.'

'We're German, as you know, and that's a German name. But we've never met such a person. I can't understand why she said that.'

'Yes, I realise. As you know already, the vehicle that hit her was a particular Ford, but nobody called Korff is registered as an owner. So that's not the connection. She must have met the mysterious Korff somewhere. As she was a well-known children's author, could that be the connection? I've quizzed her illustrator, and she knows nothing. So where could Ursula have gone?'

'I'll get her diaries. She listed everywhere she went for book launches and talks. Her record goes back to when she began writing. Later, once her books were published, *she became very active in promoting them*. One of those diaries may provide a clue.'

'Great. Is there any chance I could borrow them?'

'Certainly. Have them all, if it helps.'

He was as good as his word, and following a shared cup of tea and every reassurance she could truthfully give, Lillian had Ursula's diaries in her briefcase for immediate analysis back at the police station. On her short drive back, she uttered a heartfelt prayer of her own.

'Please, dear God, give me a clue.'

With her office door closed and instructions to staff for no interruptions or phone calls, Lillian Boyd got to work on the voluminous diaries. Starting years back, with a separate edition for each new calendar year, they listed every book launch, planning discussion and publishing meeting that the meticulous Ursula had logged. Each edition was fortunately in English, as the educated couple had readily adapted to their new country and language.

Starting back in the late 1970s, Lillian carefully looked for clues, marking every entry that could give a lead. However, there were few. Moving into the 1980s, no mention of the enigmatic 'Korff'. Ursula was indeed active with her city and country visits. Lillian needed many a cup of coffee to help her concentrate. 'Korff' had to be in there, somewhere.

That night, her eyes tired, she had to pause, marking the spot at the end of the 1984 edition where she stopped. Nothing so far. Only two more years to go, with Ursula's final entry being her scheduled meeting with her illustrator that sad November day in 1986.

Yes, Lillian would be fresher in the morning. Driving to her rented flat in Bondi Junction, after a late snack to settle her stomach, she tumbled gratefully into bed.

As she drifted off into a blessed sleep, the thought came. *What if Korff isn't a person but a place?*

An intriguing possibility. Worth exploring tomorrow.

CHAPTER TWENTY-ONE

At the same time that Lillian was racking her brains about Ursula's mysterious last word, there was frantic activity in Lichtenberg, East Berlin. The Directorate's Special Operations Section, a veritable boiler room, was working around the clock.

To what end?

The assiduous gnomes turned out forged letters, false emails, dummy bank account statements for the Cayman Islands, shell company records and miscellaneous deceptive documents.

One name featured prominently: Prime Minister Bob Hawke.

Discretionary funds the prime minister had access to appeared to have been deposited in his 'account' with the Caymans. Especially ALP campaign funds for vulnerable seats. A reading of all this would give the ALP no chance of winning the next election, due in 1990.

It was an absolute scandal. You would have to assume Hawke had embezzled all that money to set himself up abroad in some tax haven without an extradition treaty with Australia.

Shocking.

'Excellent work!' Otto Dreschner congratulated the forgers. 'Magnificent!'

They'd do the trick, alright. Not for nothing was the special section nicknamed the 'counterfeit room'.

The final step in the process was to place all the material, carefully given a last check, into the diplomatic satchel for couriering to Red Hill, Canberra, with a confirming phone call from Dreschner.

'Ambassador, it's on its way. Make sure you alert Comrade Richter... er, Rickard, to take charge once it arrives and do his homework carefully. Used effectively, it will be dynamite.'

'Certainly, Comrade Dreschner. Exactly as you ask.'

Well, well, well. Bob Hawke, preparing to live the life of Riley in an untouchable tax haven? No doubt with cigars and booze on tap!

An uncharitable thought concerning a dedicated prime minister who had actually given up alcohol before being elected.

However, the GDR regime did not concern itself with such niceties. Forget the truth – appearances would be everything.

Klaus and Xanthe were having, if not an argument, a difference of opinion. All over his 'secret life' and unwillingness to commit.

'Klaus, you don't come around when you say you will. Why do you keep going off on travels? It can't always be your PhD research!'

'Xanthe, stop pressuring me. Are you worried about another woman? There's certainly nobody else!'

At least that part was true.

'Alright, then! I just want to know you care...'

He assured her he did, but a little voice told her something was up.

Xanthe Young's sixth sense was spot on.

CHAPTER TWENTY-TWO

Eagerly resuming her analysis of the last two years of Ursula's diary entries the next morning, Lillian seemed to have a fresh lead.

Yes, there in mid-1985 were the author's listed visits to book launches in a series of north coast towns. Goodness, she'd visited Ballina, Yamba, Maclean, Grafton, Coffs Harbour and Port Macquarie. She sure had a work ethic!

Ursula seemed to have divided the state into regions and then blitzed each locality. Edrick, Gertie, Bluey and Goldie really got a workout. There must have been hundreds of delighted children. No doubt saddened now the last edition would be forever unfinished.

In her mind, Lillian sounded out the names. Ballina, Yamba… She stopped at Coffs Harbour.

'Coffs… Korff?'

She checked Sophie van den Bosch's witness statement. The interviewing constable had asked if Ursula had 'wanted to cough', perhaps? A dying reflex?

No, Sophie was adamant. The word was clearly 'Korff'. So Lillian, on a hunch, did a computer check.

There was the answer, as clear as a bell.

In 1847, Captain John Korff had sheltered in that north coast harbour, later called Korff's Harbour. Over time, it became naturally anglicised to Coffs Harbour, by which name that attractive tourist town was still known.

'That's it! Ursula was connected to Coffs!'

A eureka moment.

Lillian's mind raced. Why was this so critical? Ursula's 1985 visit there was the only one recorded.

A phone call to Jonas Schneider confirmed she had never returned to that town nor been there before. So why was that her dying word, repeated for emphasis? A clue poor Ursula trusted compassionate young Sophie, a good Samaritan stranger, would pass on?

After hanging up, Lillian hoped a strong cup of coffee would stimulate her brain cells. Yes, phone him back.

'Sorry to trouble you again, Mr Schneider. Can you think of anything Ursula might have done in Coffs Harbour to emphasise the word Korff?'

Sadly, he couldn't. At least not then.

Ten minutes later, he returned her phone call.

'Detective Sergeant Boyd, I've just remembered. When Ursula returned from that north coast trip, she told me she'd had a minor incident on leaving the Coffs Harbour library. She'd bumped into a man and lost her pile of books. She was worried about their being damaged. The man had kindly picked them up for her and helped her to her car. He was definitely a stranger – she'd never met him before. Funnily enough, she said he had a slight German accent.'

'OK, enter a mysterious stranger. That could be a lead. But why say Korff?'

'No idea, sorry. That's all I know.'

'Thanks, Mr Schneider. I'll follow it up.'

Lillian resolved to do just that.

\- - -

The Pacific Highway north from Sydney in 1988 was far from an ideal major route, Lillian opined as she drove. It definitely needed to be a double carriageway all the way to the Queensland border. There had been improvements, but far more remained to be done. Nevertheless, she made good time, with two comfort stops. The last stretch from Nambucca Heads onwards was frustratingly slow, but Lillian knew her goal was in sight.

Carefully observing the speed limit as she arrived in Coffs, Lillian soon noticed ahead of her the town library in Castle Street, where it had been located for the last fifteen years. The building was part of a complex which included the tourist information centre. A phone call made before departing Sydney had confirmed Chief Librarian Tahlia Grace would be on duty until late that afternoon. Lillian had risen early at 4 a.m. to ensure she'd be there in time.

'Hello, Ms Grace. I trust you can spare me a few minutes?'

'As much time as you need, Detective Sergeant. I gather this is an important matter.'

'It sure is. A cold case involving a Sydney hit-and-run death in 1986.'

Over a much-needed cup of tea, Lillian filled Tahlia in on all the salient facts. She was all ears and quite forthcoming.

'I remember poor Ursula Schneider quite clearly, and her presentation that day in July 1985. A lovely woman, very warm and friendly. She loved the kids and related wonderfully to the parents. Gave out little gifts, you know. Fortunately not lollies, so we didn't have to worry about grubby fingers touching the books. Librarians appreciate that sort of thing.'

'I can understand that.'

'It was a very successful meeting, although Ursula had brought rather too many books, hence her unfortunate minor accident as she left.'

'Did you happen to see it?'

'In fact, I did. I had offered to help carry her surplus books to her car outside. She declined my offer, but I was still a bit concerned so watched as she left.'

'So did you see her bump into that stranger?'

'I sure did, and was just about to race outside to help when he considerately helped her. She seemed quite relieved. As there was nothing more for me to do, I just watched him walk off and saw her drive away. Nothing was left behind, and she clearly wasn't hurt, so I took no further action.'

'Fair enough. Is that all?'

'Oh, sorry, I almost forgot. We're big on occupational health and safety, so I completed a brief incident report to hopefully avoid anything like that happening again. After that, we insisted on a staff member helping visiting authors to their car. Duty of care, you know.'

'So that report is still on file?'

'Yes, it is. Do you want a copy?'

Lillian appreciated Tahlia's helpful attitude and readily accepted. A photocopy of the report was in her hands minutes later. She noted the helpful stranger had then gone further down Castle Street. That gave her something to go on.

'Can I do anything else to help?'

Lillian was sorry not all her contacts were as obliging and helpful as Tahlia Grace.

'No, I think that's all for now, unless there's anything else we haven't discussed that's occurred to you. So I'll get back to you if there are any leads. I'll now get cracking and do my own follow-up.'

Tahlia did seem eager to add something.

'Detective Sergeant, we did get information stating poor Ursula Schneider had passed away but had no idea of the cause. So we reluctantly deleted her from our authors list. I got her home address and next of kin from our records and sent her husband a sympathy card on behalf of the library.'

'Thank you, that was very kind.' Lillian, a good judge of character, felt this would have been a typical act of empathy from the chief librarian.

'Not at all.'

'One final thing. We're puzzled as to why she said "Korff" as she died.'

Lillian told Tahlia how she'd found the story of Captain John Korff.

'Before Ursula began her author's talk, she listened to another presentation on the history of the founding of the town. She was intrigued by the German connection with Korff.'

'Interesting. Thank you.'

Taking her leave, Lillian checked the incident scene and walked in the direction the stranger would have followed on the day in question. Castle was a fairly short street, with only a few shops, which were now starting to close. More to do tomorrow. The shopkeepers wouldn't appreciate having their closing-down interrupted and might be more amenable tomorrow. She'd try them then.

Back in her car, Lillian found her night's accommodation in the nearby pre-booked Surf and Sands Motel. After a much-needed bowling club dinner, she retired to her motel room, reviewed her plans for the next day and turned in as soon as possible. It had been a long day.

She was starting to make progress.

CHAPTER TWENTY-THREE

Fresh from an excellent sleep and buoyed by a full breakfast she'd chosen from the motel menu, Lillian began her check of the Castle Street shops the stranger might have visited and then continued down to Vernon Street at the end. She eliminated those that had been opened only recently, or had a new proprietor. The local chamber of commerce and tourist information centre were helpful there.

'No, I have no recollection of anything that day, not the foggiest idea,' was the all-too-frequent reply. The 'stranger' was evidently some sort of shadowy figure, hardly real.

Yet he was.

Feeling discouraged and not a little footsore, when she mentioned the 'German' yet again, Len in a small hardware store seemed somewhat more helpful than others, bored with her enquiries.

'A German, you reckon? No idea myself, but Wal three doors down – you, know, the union man – I'm pretty sure he's German. Speaks great English, but there's an accent. I reckon he might know. But almost three years ago? It'll be a long shot.'

'Thanks, Len.'

Yes, a long shot, but worth trying.

There was the sign out the front, '*Allied Rural Industries*'. In she went.

He needed some prompting to give his name, Wal Newell. German? A definite name change there. There were some union pamphlets on the counter, and she took one, at which he frowned but said nothing.

Showing her badge and outlining her enquiry, she detected immediate resistance. Getting anything out of Wal Newell was like pulling teeth. The contrast with the other shopkeepers, even the bored ones, was palpable. He was the other end of the sociability scale from the delightful Tahlia Grace, just a short distance up the road.

He eventually conceded he kept a visitors record, for union purposes. Yes, he had the 1985 diary. That's where the co-operation stopped.

'Do you have a warrant?'

Lillian's hackles rose immediately. 'Why would I need a warrant for a simple attendance check? What are you hiding?'

From Newell's body language, it was evident he realised he'd overplayed his hand. Reluctantly, he relented and produced the 1985 diary.

Finding the relevant July day, and knowing the approximate time, there was only one entry. The initials 'K. Z.' That person was the last visitor.

'So, who is K. Z.? Why didn't he write down his full name?'

Newell was on the defensive.

'I can't remember, and I'm not sure I made that entry. There are other staff here sometimes. I may not have been on duty that day.' His German accent was becoming more obvious with the stress. What was he hiding?

She tried a new tack. 'OK, tell me about your union.'

He relaxed a bit at that and gave a quick spiel. Lillian nodded appreciatively, doing her best to keep him on side for now. Studying the pamphlet, it was obviously a very left-wing union, almost radical. Based here in a regional area because of the union's nature and workforce. So that's how he was politically – left-wing? Worth noting. The pamphlet gave his position with a brief bio, confirming what Newell had just told her.

Realising there was something left to discover here but unable to proceed further, she excused herself as civilly as possible from the recalcitrant Wal Newell and drove to Coffs Harbour Police Station. Prior to leaving Sydney, she had phoned ahead to let them know she'd be in their area following an enquiry. The officer in charge confirmed she was welcome to visit for any support she'd need.

After taking some refreshment and setting herself up in a borrowed office, Lillian did some summing up. *Here we have three people of German origin. The road victim, the uncooperative union leader and the mysterious stranger, 'K. Z.' What's the connection?*

Ursula and her husband were refugees from East Germany. She'd check with Immigration as to where Newell had come from. She had the facts on him, but K. Z. was still an unknown factor.

Immigration undertook to get back to her as soon as possible and did so within half an hour. Walter Neumann, now Wal Newell, had migrated from Bamberg in West Germany several years before. His settlement file revealed he was an active union man who had immediately joined Allied Rural Industries as a rank-and-file member, proceeded up the ladder and become union leader five years ago. Newell was a keen member of the Australian Labor Party and regularly attended their events.

Lillian thanked the Immigration clerk and was about to hang up when he interrupted.

'Oh, just one more thing, in case it's important. When he was interviewed by our official in the Australian Embassy in Bonn, that man made a notation on Neumann's file. It says, "*Speaks with an accent consistent with the GDR – the German Democratic Republic – rather than Bamberg in Bavaria*". It seems our official was a bit of a linguist. However, Neumann insisted he was from Bamberg and had all necessary supporting papers. There were no grounds for further action.'

'Well, that's certainly interesting! Many thanks for your help.'

She hung up, intrigued. An East German victim. A left-wing person here in Coffs Harbour suspected of coming from the same area, which he denied, and an enigmatic 'K. Z.'

Lillian Boyd knew the old saying. Three similar events were no coincidence. It all signified danger.

Prepare for enemy action.

CHAPTER TWENTY-FOUR

Bill and Maureen Young were at their wits' end with poor Xanthe. Right now, she was sobbing inconsolably in her bedroom. Klaus had forgotten her birthday yesterday and missed their date night to celebrate!

'Love, there must be an explanation. Maybe his research delayed him somewhere. We'll sort it out.'

There's only so much caring parents can do in such a situation, and they racked their brains for an answer. When she agreed to come out for a lunch with them later, they were relieved. For now, she was staying in her room.

'She's so sensitive, but she's right. He had no reason to miss her birthday when he'd promised her so much.'

A brilliant young woman, highly educated, with a career laid out before her, Xanthe's one weakness was to be too trusting of men. Klaus was becoming a disappointment, and they decided to do their best to offer their daughter some counselling in the hope of getting her to cut the emotional link. Klaus Ziegler needed to be dumped.

Problem-solvers, they reviewed where the relationship had gone wrong. Why did he let her down? It was unlikely to be another woman, because he travelled to different places, especially Western Australia and the NSW north coast. Canberra featured as well.

The next option was a financial scam, promptly ruled out. He was never short of cash and was generous with it, buying her presents. Klaus seemed uninterested in the Youngs' standard of living. He did have a gambling problem, but when he lost on the horses, it didn't seem to worry him. While being a drinker, he wasn't dependent on it, so not an alcoholic. Drug user? Apparently not. Xanthe had often said she'd never seen any evidence, nor was Klaus ever 'high'. It seemed unlikely he was organising a drug ring.

His study pattern was highly erratic, and he'd sometimes told Xanthe Dr Wexall was 'on his case'. Funny, when that happened, Klaus would disappear to Canberra, and soon afterwards there would appear a body of research.

The most troubling aspect of all this, apart from the emotional disappointment Xanthe was suffering, was the man's inconsistent stories.

Bill was clever at noting them whenever Klaus came over for dinner. Where he'd grown up, details of his parents and siblings. His early education. Nothing major, but subtle variations, especially if he'd had something to drink. It was cause for concern. Klaus was careful whenever politics came up as a dinner subject. But there were occasional flashes of anger which he couldn't control whenever some aspect of government policy was discussed. Curious.

They analysed the options again, making notes and coming up with a final assessment.

'So, what do you reckon, Bill?'

Maureen wanted an answer and could always trust her husband's judgment. It had been the same when managing their old Mudgee property.

Bill pursed his lips and looked her straight in the eye, holding her gaze until she was somewhat uncomfortable.

'I reckon he's a foreign spy!'

The desk sergeant at Strathfield Police Station realised the determined middle-aged couple in front of him meant business, emphasising they had some urgent information and needed time with the most senior officer available. He immediately contacted the area inspector, who arrived promptly. A vacant office was quickly made available.

'Please, take a seat, Mr and Mrs Young. How can I help you?'

They shared their concerns about Klaus Ziegler. The inspector looked quizzical.

'I'm afraid we need evidence, not just a suspicion, before we can take action. What has this Klaus Ziegler done?'

'Inspector, we realise there's a lack of actual evidence, but please look at his track record. Strange absences, a funny travel pattern, inconsistent academic record. He's not a normal student!'

'Yes, yes. I gather you're very concerned he's let your daughter down romantically. That's not an offence, of course, unless he's committed a crime along with it. A money scam or the like.'

'Nothing like that, no.'

'So let's monitor the situation and see what develops. I'll log this as a general report and circulate his name to those likely to need to follow up. I'll leave the Australian Federal Police and ASIO – you know, the Australian Security Intelligence Organisation – out of it for now, but that will be a later option should some evidence arise. Mr and Mrs Young, thank you for your time. Rest assured we'll keep the matter of Mr Ziegler under constant review.'

'Yeah, sure.'

Giving each other a knowing glance, they left the inspector.

It was back home to cheer Xanthe up with a visit to a Strathfield's favourite establishment, the Golden Dragon. A lovely yum cha lunch would be just what the doctor ordered.

CHAPTER TWENTY-FIVE

As 1988 unfolded, Admiral Vladimir Rostov was delighted with the progress of his build-up of the Soviet Union's Pacific Fleet. The pride of the fleet, the aircraft carrier *Tbilisi*, was at anchor off Vladivostok, that window to the far east, so important to the Pacific Ocean and the thrust his homeland – Mother Russia – would soon make into that greatest ocean on planet Earth, up till now seen as the playground of their capitalist international rival, the United States of America.

Thoroughly complementing the Peter the Great Gulf in Primorsky Krai, plus two strategic locations on the Kamchatka Peninsula, the newly expanded bases in the Kuril Islands were about to serve their purpose magnificently. Snatched from Imperial Japan in 1945 in the dying days of the Second World War, the Kurils were essential to Russian expansion into the Pacific.

'Magnificent, absolutely magnificent!' the admiral congratulated himself. 'General Secretary Gorbachev will be delighted.' Or if he wasn't – too bad! Rostov worked to his own agenda and had no truck with the growing policy of 'glasnost and perestroika', openness and restructuring, the new Russian leader had brought in.

Mikhail Gorbachev now occupied the supreme Soviet position, having obtained the post on Chernenko's death in 1985.

Another general secretary to be circumvented. A speed bump in the road, according to the ambitious Rostov. Yes, he had his own aims and wanted a position much higher than admiral in the years ahead. He particularly disliked Gorbachev and his agenda. He'd do his best to sabotage anything the new appointee stood for. But for now, there was the task that awaited…

There before Rostov, as well as the splendid *Tbilisi*, was the expanded fleet. Battlecruisers, cruisers, destroyers, frigates, corvettes, submarines, both nuclear and conventionally powered… as far as the eye could see. Once fully deployed, the glorious Pacific Fleet would set the Yanks back on their heels.

He'd see them confined to Hawaii if it was the last thing he did.

Rostov's particular interest was the battlecruiser *Kalinin*, dedicated for a special mission that was now coming up. There had been hush-hush Kremlin conversations with one of their loyal allies and the details specified as both parties laid their plans. Anticipating a successful outcome, it would be a master stroke.

Rostov called a meeting of trusted subordinates as the spring sunshine outside, a clear omen, bathed Vladivostok in a healthy glow. There were various business matters to discuss and approve.

'Comrades, I want the *Kalinin* spick and span before departure on our important mission. Get the men to scrub the decks till they can see their faces reflected. When we succeed, it will all have been worth it.'

There was an appreciative murmur.

He then moved to the main item on the agenda, the naval budget. With his accountant fidgeting nervously on the edge of his chair, Rostov sensed some reluctance. General Secretary Gorbachev, who had inherited Chernenko's budget, was of the same opinion, that he well knew. The new fleet might well be impressive… but the cost!

Announcing the item, it was time for Rostov to launch a pre-emptive strike. With a theatrical gesture to the vast Pacific Fleet moored outside, he did so.

'The current budget? Hang the expense, what's one hundred billion roubles between friends? Cheap at twice the price!'

Indeed. If you say so, Admiral.

CHAPTER TWENTY-SIX

Back in Randwick, Lillian was motivated to prepare for some unseen enemy action but was unsure exactly how to do it. She was on the verge of preparing a general memo for the widest possible circulation when a nugget of information came in, originating from Strathfield Police Station. In essence, it stated, *'Suspicions raised about private overseas student Klaus Ziegler of 10 Underpass Street, Glebe, studying at… No present evidence, but stay alert.'*

'Klaus Ziegler! The mysterious K. Z.!'

It had to be no coincidence.

Yes, he had been the registered owner of exactly the Ford Falcon make which had struck and killed Ursula Schneider. The vehicle had left his ownership shortly afterwards and there was then no record of it. Why hadn't that been followed up on at the time? He now owned a different make, a Holden Commodore. Really? A Ford owner turning to a Holden? That had to be deliberate.

She needed Ziegler's background.

'Mr Findlay, this is Detective Sergeant Lillian Boyd of Randwick Police…'

Kendrick Findlay quickly pulled up Klaus Ziegler's file, with the various academic warnings. He'd taken his time to complete his master's degree and was making slow progress with his PhD studies. A subsequent call to Felix Wexall confirmed it. Research handed in right after Canberra trips was significant.

So where did he go in Canberra? She had a hunch.

'ASIO, this is...'

She was put through to the Embassy Unit. With ASIO officers checking on frequent visitors to 'hostile embassies', there was bound to be a log.

There was.

Ziegler's vehicle often visited both the GDR Embassy chancery in Red Hill and the Farrer residence. After such visits, he handed in his academic research for scrutiny by Dr Wexall. The rotten cheat! Although that was the least of their problems.

The evidence was starting to accumulate. Klaus Ziegler was an East German spy.

Oh, she'd crack the hit-and-run case, all right. But there was more at stake than that.

Far more.

Lillian's next step was to analyse his travels. Who was he visiting and where? Western Australia – Perth – occupied quite a bit of his time. Who did he see there? Lillian phoned a contact she had with WA Police. He confirmed he'd get back to her.

She certainly knew about Coffs Harbour. The unhelpful Wal Newell was concealing something. Allied Rural Industries, was it? The union headquarters were probably only a front.

Firstly, she could now wrap up the hit-and-run. Ziegler was the 'helpful stranger' who bumped into Ursula that day in 1985. As she lay dying after her terrible accident in 1986, she must have recognised him from their earlier encounter. Remembering that he was German from his slight accent, and that their meeting was in Coffs Harbour, her mind threw out the German name 'Korff' as a final gesture of where she'd met him before her body gave up the ghost. That was all the poor woman could do.

Yet the police needed the evidence of the Ford. So where was it? Unlikely to have been taken to a wrecker and crushed.

The police had checked that tactic, with all Sydney wreckers' logbooks carefully scrutinised.

How about the East German Embassy? A sudden thought. ASIO would have a record. They did. Yes, soon after the Melbourne Cup Day hit-and-run, there was evidence of an embassy staff car, the same Ford. It was now using diplomatic plates for its various comings and goings. According to the log, a particular clerk, one Rudolf Wohl, regularly drove it. Gotcha!

The only problem: diplomatic immunity!

Knowing the police were onto them, the East Germans would refuse to surrender the car, or even allow a police inspection, which would reveal the frontal impact. No matter how skilful the repair job, a trained forensic investigator could always find the truth.

So Lillian would have to hold her fire for now.

What would be her plan of action? Get whatever evidence she could.

'Mr Findlay, Lillian Boyd again. May I ask you…'

Her request was granted. Kendrick Findlay sent over Klaus Ziegler's photo from the department's file. She immediately sent a copy up to Coffs Harbour Library, to Tahlia Grace.

Phoning the chief librarian a little later, there was confirmation. To the best of her recollection, he was the man she'd observed with Ursula Schneider that day in 1985. Yes, she was happy to present herself at Coffs Harbour Police Station and make a statement to be forwarded on to Randwick.

Evidence was building.

Back to her query. What was Ziegler's business with Wal Newell? And also in Western Australia?

Lillian's phone rang. It was the Northern Territory Police. She'd put out an all points bulletin to every police force throughout Australia, sending Ziegler's photo and a summary of her suspicions.

A hit from the Northern Territory.

Someone of his appearance, apart from hair colour, had

gained illegal entry to Pine Gap some time back. The offender had then somehow escaped, with no record of his identity. While Pine Gap had no photo, a later interview of the American staff produced a general description. Now, with the photo, definitely Klaus Ziegler.

Lillian Boyd was heartened. The mills of justice indeed turn slowly, but they grind exceedingly fine.

CHAPTER TWENTY-SEVEN

June, early winter, was hardly the peak of the tourist season in the southern climes of Tasmania, visitors then being somewhat infrequent. Not so at the beginning of June in 1988. There was a decided influx, all of them having a special purpose in mind rather than tourism. Some would eschew any travel beyond their purpose, eager to return home immediately once their business trip was concluded. Such was the lure of warmer parts of Australia. Everywhere else was further north than the beautiful capital of that island state, Hobart, and more hours of winter sunshine would be a given. The winter solstice was fast approaching.

However, some visitors would stay on, eager to avail themselves of the charm of historic Hobart, perhaps grasping the opportunity to travel rather further afield. A trip a little to the south to Bruny Island was an attractive option. A drive somewhat northwards to the Tasman Peninsula, featuring the former convict settlement of Port Arthur. Who knows, they could then continue on up the eye-catching east coast, with Swansea and Bicheno on the itinerary. None of those enticing locations would disappoint.

Considering all of this, Steve Kavanagh, who would chair the coming conference proceedings, nevertheless eliminated them from his thoughts, delightful as an east coast odyssey would be.

He was too focussed on the immediate task before him. Even so, he briefly allowed his attention to wander one final time.

When it's all over, I'll book myself on a Hobart Historic Lunch Cruise, I reckon. Or a cruise right up the Derwent. Under the Tasman Bridge, past Selfs Point, Dowsing Point, beyond Dogshear Point… Great! Then fit in a trip up Mount Wellington as well.

But back to reality. Steve succeeded at last in eliminating such distractions and now concentrated on the task ahead.

Must confirm the conference agenda once more when notifications close at 6 p.m.

That was two hours away, with business due to commence the next day precisely at 9 a.m. *Now, what's this special motion? Seems curious. Quite unusual. Better have another look at it. It's got support from another quarter.*

Steve was meticulous about anything related to his career.

His background was in journalism, having graduated with a qualification in communication studies from the University of Newcastle. Starting right away as a fully-fledged reporter, he'd gained a position with one of the Hunter Valley newspapers and was often seconded to other media locations in the area. He loved the print medium. His seminal editorial on the perils of 'renegade truck drivers' was picked up by the state Department of Main Roads, with his safety recommendations incorporated into the department's action project.

Glad I could help, his thoughts ran when that memory returned. Yes, his plan for a computerised record, point-to-point tracking cameras, detailed logbooks, compulsory rest breaks, stringent random breath and drug tests and the like were adopted, some right away, others when technology was available. Get the drunks and druggies off the road!

Well, that was then, this is now.

A keen union man, influenced by industrial matters during his life in Newcastle, the 'Steel City', he'd joined his professional association and was now, following a succession of promotions, its general secretary. The head. He'd been nominated to chair tomorrow's meeting with support from the highest level.

Do a final check. The agenda has to be in apple-pie order.

He was right to do so, as this was the year's big event, the 1988 Australian Labor Party's Thirty-Eighth National Conference.

An internal body of the ALP, the conference was the party's highest representative body of its various branches. Held every three years since the 1970s, this year it was scheduled for Hobart, starting on 9 June. It was always held in different states to be more democratic – equal, if you like. The aim was to draft a statement of party policy, the National Platform. Decisions would be implemented by the National Executive, with twenty members elected to do this.

This time, Steve Kavanagh was to be chairman, a high honour. How good that his professional association would now have the recognition it deserved! As well as ALP members of parliament, including Prime Minister Hawke, there were rank-and-file delegated members and union heads, such as himself. This time, someone else would represent his professional association – he would have to be impartial. More than that, especially alert.

Yep, I know Hawkie is worried about the Labor Left, and he'll get stuck into them if they don't try it first. Be on guard!

Ah, yes – the political rivalry between the Labor Right and Left. Some saw it as democracy in action, others as the bane of the party, officially described as 'a modern social democratic party'.

Keep control, Steve thought.

The Thirty-Eighth National Conference due to commence at 9 a.m. tomorrow would be very important, the last one before the next federal election, due in two years' time. Nineteen ninety would be a watershed year. There'd been three election victories for the Hawke government so far. Would there be a fourth?

Well, we'll find out. For now, watch Hawkie and the Labor Left.

Steve Kavanagh would soon discover the Labor Left would be the least of his worries.

Very much the least.

CHAPTER TWENTY-EIGHT

Dr Felix Wexall was concerned about his PhD student's progress and determined to counsel him about it. Ziegler was slow to produce research, which in any case was of mediocre quality. Yet when he was criticised on that basis, there would be a sudden input after a rumoured trip to Canberra. Ziegler attempted to justify his Canberra trips on the basis of the 'political' nature of the federal capital, which cut some ice with Wexall. For a while, at least.

'Right, let's have another look at his data.'

Sadly, it seemed inadequate and, frankly, not up to any academic standard. Klaus Ziegler wouldn't be awarded his doctorate any time soon. Worse still, Wexall detected a change in style from Ziegler's earlier findings. Subtle variations. Surely he couldn't be engaging in plagiarism? If it was that – disgraceful!

So what happened in Canberra?

Equally concerning, there'd been a police enquiry about him. What was the man up to? Time for another interview. Ziegler was far from prompt in replying but eventually agreed to a meeting.

'Klaus, I'm worried about your progress. Your work is sloppy and your data less than first-rate. Frankly, my friend, your doctoral studies are in question.'

Curse that Rudolf, Ziegler thought. *He's not up to the job.*

'I apologise, Doctor. I'll do my best to lift my game.'

'Pleased to hear it. By the way, the police have been enquiring about you. What's that about?'

Ziegler was now fully alert. Who was onto him?

'I have no idea. What did they say?'

Wexall mentally chastised himself for being indiscreet and back-pedalled.

'Sorry, I forget the details. Nothing I can recall. I assume all's OK?'

It was far from OK in Ziegler's mind.

'Oh, it may have been a speeding fine. Perhaps I should've been faster to pay it.' His mind was racing.

'Alright, Klaus, let's leave it there. Bye for now.'

'Bye, Dr Wexall.'

It really would be goodbye. Dr Wexall could go jump.

Leaving the university, Ziegler realised the game was almost up. He'd better get going before they were onto him. Was it his Pine Gap escapade catching up with him? Or the Melbourne Cup Day hit-and-run? Or surveillance of the embassy?

He didn't know, but the clock was ticking. In any case, he had to head north, whether they were after him or not. Time was marching on, and Hobart was about to happen.

Get ready for the climax.

He drove straight back to Glebe and packed what he needed, knowing the rest would be available and well-prepared at his destination. Now to laying a false trail. Carefully not drawing any attention to himself, he drove directly to Sydney Airport's domestic parking area, got a parking ticket on entry and chose the 'long stay' section. Next, the job of finding alternate transport. There had to be many targets.

Nearby was an early model Toyota Camry which resisted his entry for mere seconds. Falling back on his forest camp training, Ziegler was able to hot-wire it, the motor responding by firing comfortingly. He calmly drove it to the exit booth, paying cash to the bored attendant using the parking ticket the owner had considerately left on the dashboard. A bonus was an almost full tank of petrol.

Delighted with his own ability to make the most of a tricky situation, Ziegler was soon on the Pacific Highway heading north out of Sydney. He congratulated himself as he thought of the final touch. When any cops found the Holden, there on the front seat were some handwritten notes indicating a trip to Adelaide. They'd scratch their heads over that one. He could just hear them. *'Adelaide? What the heck's he doing there?'*

Oh, the cops here and interstate would run in circles for days. He laughed out loud. Sure, they'd check the flights, but would assume travel under an alias and interview every passenger. That'd keep them very busy!

With the extra cover of night, the Toyota moved relentlessly north, an almost ecstatic driver at the wheel. The deprived owner could be away for days, and the mission would climax successfully well before he even knew his car was gone.

As for any nosy cops, they'd never think of Allied Rural Industries in Coffs Harbour. In any case, that's where Ziegler needed to be. Come hell or high water.

CHAPTER TWENTY-NINE

With a tactical response team in support, Lillian Boyd raided Ziegler's Glebe flat, only to find it almost empty of his possessions. Neighbours confirmed he'd cleared out two days before. She put out an all points bulletin urging his arrest on suspicion of the 1986 hit-and-run, fully aware that was just the tip of the iceberg. The registration number of his Holden was put on a watchlist.

The raid was justified by information from the Western Australian Police detailing his visits to Ernie Rickard, member for Mainwaring, indicating suspicious activity. The police would follow up with Rickard, who for now was unavailable.

At her desk at Randwick Police Station, Lillian considered her options. Certainly, there'd been progress with the investigation, which revealed a three-way conspiracy between Klaus Ziegler, Wal Newell and Ern Rickard. What on earth were they up to? And when would they strike? The first conspirator was supposedly a student. The second a union head. The third a member of parliament. She sketched this out.

A constable phoned through an update. Klaus Ziegler's car had been discovered at Sydney Airport with evidence he'd flown to Adelaide. Or so it seemed.

'Adelaide, you reckon?' she exclaimed out loud. 'We'll see about that. He's sure gone somewhere. Come on, girl – join the dots!'

Lillian's eye caught the heading of today's Sydney Morning Herald newspaper casually tossed on her desk. '*ALP Annual Conference Starts*.' There were all the details, the location, the delegates. Yes, it had to be that. A Labor MP from Western Australia and a union general secretary were there for sure. No way would they miss it. Probably with their mysterious henchman as well.

'That's it – Hobart! They're up to no good there!' You could almost hear the cogs turning. 'But exactly what?'

And what were her options? Phoning conference security to alert them to be careful was one. That trio could try anything. *Think, think, think!*

First, a strong cup of coffee to get the neurons firing.

Then, pick up the phone.

Meeting up at their accommodation, the Derwent River Motel, following their separate early morning flights to Hobart, Wal Newell and Ern Rickard were keen to go over their planned strategy. Carefully analysing the pack of information for the coup – the forged documents, Cayman Islands bank statements, email copies and the like – was the first step.

Steve Kavanagh had been alerted to a special item that was on the agenda for the final day, lodged according to conference rules. Their daring strike. They'd locked in the timing. Yes, done. They expected the chairman to be putty in their hands.

With all in readiness, it was almost surreal the two conspirators then decided a tour of Tasmania's capital was the next thing on their personal schedule. Sure, explore Hobart on the red decker. Feeling relaxed with their preparations done, and with the rest of the day at leisure, off they went.

The ninety-minute loop. Hop on, hop off with twenty stops. Battery Point, Wrest Point Casino, the Female Factory and the botanical gardens the high points. Perhaps a stop at the casino for a flutter.

Why not? Don't let the capitalists have all the fun.

Comrades also need their day off.

CHAPTER THIRTY

Ever since the *Kalinin* had departed Primorsky Krai, Vladivostok, the captain, had steered his course remorselessly southwards.

Departing in late spring, on a blustery but sunny day, with the trees and gardens ashore bursting forth with greenery following the long winter, the battle cruiser had crossed into the tropics, then the equator, and still there was a distance ahead before it reached its goal deep within the southern hemisphere.

Aboard, apart from the usual complement of Soviet Navy crew, were Admiral Rostov himself and two special guests. These men had flown to Moscow for a personal briefing with a particular KGB officer, one of Rostov's protégés, before travelling on the considerable distance to that great city of the Russian far east, Vladivostok. Rostov was 'in' with the KGB, thanks to this officer who would do his bidding, and had ordered details be kept 'hush-hush' from Mikhail Gorbachev, who knew nothing about this special mission. Time enough for him to be informed when it climaxed. Then events would force him to support it and be in Rostov's pocket.

'Comrade, I tell you, our plans are well prepared,' the senior of the two, Horst Moltke, had assured the Soviet secret service officer. 'Our three operatives have been carefully selected and impeccably trained. We've scrutinised their mission, which is minutely timed. You can rely on us!'

His subordinate, Otto Dreschner, nodded in agreement.

'Thank you, comrades. I await news of your achievement. In that event, Admiral Rostov will be ready to play his part. Let's drink to your mission's success!'

The two Stasi men happily agreed. Then it was on to the airport and the next part of their journey eastwards...

Now the *Kalinin* was much closer to its goal, but there were still many kilometres to go. Having traversed the Coral Sea and steered clear of the Great Barrier Reef with the Tropic of Capricorn behind them, those aboard once more became aware of the start of the southern winter, with the long days of the Russian spring having given way to the shortened daylight of the month heralding the southern solstice, which was not so many days ahead.

Curious to go within a couple of weeks from almost summer to winter. Few of those on board, apart from the admiral, had previously visited the southern hemisphere.

Entertaining his two Stasi guests over dinner, Admiral Rostov speculated happily as to how they would be received at their destination.

'Comrades Moltke and Dreschner, I've had my new dress uniform specially laundered! The capitalists who see it will be impressed! As you may know, I've previously met my counterparts in the British and American navies, and we were on an equal footing. This time, shall we say, your esteemed socialist country and mine will be in an – er – rather superior position. I trust our hosts will see our visit as an extension of their recent bicentennial celebrations. Ours isn't a tall ship, of course, but certainly one with more firepower, which no doubt will impress them. I wonder if they'll put on fireworks? Comrades, I can't wait!'

Neither could his Stasi guests. What a thought – fireworks!

Klaus Ziegler had sent back detailed photos of the presumed venue, one fit for esteemed guests such as them. A stunning location, exactly matching Rostov's rank, with a view to die for. Emphasising what it and the mansion next to it were called, they pointed at his uniform and laughed. How apt. Even the Stasi could make an in-joke, it seemed.

Horst Moltke couldn't resist adding, 'Admiral, let's charge our glasses and drink to our success!'

There was no argument with that.

Had Admiral Rostov, the Stasi heads and his eager crew been aware of the efficiency of Australia's maritime surveillance activities, they would have been less confident. The presence of the *Kalinin* was noted from the time it steamed through the Coral Sea. With its tell-tale shape and configuration, it was readily identified as a Soviet battle cruiser. The Royal Australian Navy was alerted.

Watch and wait.

Immediately suspecting Klaus Ziegler might not be in Hobart but may have another mission, Lillian Boyd put in a call to whoever was chairing the conference.

Steve Kavanagh.

'Mr Kavanagh? Detective Sergeant Lillian Boyd of Randwick Police. This is important...'

He remembered her name. She'd previously phoned conference security, and they'd alerted him. A useful tipoff, in fact...

Day two of the conference was just about to begin. However, Steve had time to do a quick check. Yes, Walter Newell and Ern Rickard had certainly arrived. So there was a query about them? Well, he'd follow up on that as a top priority the moment there was a break in proceedings. Or he'd call a special recess. He had a long list of essential contacts.

As for Klaus Ziegler, there was no evidence of anyone by that name having registered. It would've been highly irregular if he had, because he wasn't an ALP member and was unknown to the party. He most definitely wasn't a certified press representative.

'Detective Sergeant, he's not here, no way. Please excuse me, we're about to start…'

Lillian left him to it.

She did her calculations. Ziegler wasn't in Adelaide – that was a blind. Nor was he in Hobart. He could still be in Sydney somewhere, but what would be the point? He'd vacated his flat in Glebe and knew they were onto him. Unlikely he would have gone to Western Australia, certainly not by plane, and had he stolen a car, it would've taken too long.

So where was he?

Then the phone call came through – *'Please check your computer'*. She'd alerted all the police forces and other authorities about the wanted man, urging them to report any relevant information.

Following up on her computer, she scrolled through various suspicious references. A curious one: Marine Surveillance reported a mysterious Soviet battle cruiser steaming south, giving seven locations, beginning off the Queensland coast.

Lillian found a map and with a pen joined all those spottings to pinpoint the ship's course. The trajectory became clear. With a ruler, she found, if not its goal, then where it would all but intersect with the Australian coast – soon, very soon. It could be berthing there or heading to whatever port of call it chose.

She whistled. Wow! The penny well and truly dropped.

Checking she had all her appointments, especially her Smith and Wesson .38 revolver fully loaded with spare ammunition, she booked a plane ticket to her destination with a rental car waiting. Then urged a constable to rush her to Sydney Airport. Before leaving, she phoned ahead for them to hold the plane.

'Put your foot down, Constable. Burn some rubber. Let's have a siren all the way!'

'Yes, ma'am!'

He was happy to comply. The Sydney traffic parted like the waters of the Red Sea.

CHAPTER THIRTY-ONE

The Thirty-Eighth Australian Labor Party Conference had been underway for two days, with the delegates having settled in to the usual argy-bargy. The Labor Right and Left factions had done the usual sniping at each other. Prime Minister Bob Hawke was comfortable enough with the proceedings, ably chaired by Steve Kavanagh.

So far, the feared push from the Left hadn't eventuated, at least not to any worrying extent.

The prime minister was grateful Labor policy wasn't for the National Conference to elect the party's parliamentary leaders. Although there was always the possibility someone would try it on.

'Time's up, delegate!' Steve would call, if a particular speaker spoke too long or failed to show respect. They didn't argue.

The unions, rank-and-file members and serving members of parliament attended. All were entitled to speak, provided permission had been obtained from the Chair, with the necessary paperwork lodged beforehand. When it came to a vote, this usually happened on a factional basis. Bob Hawke was confident the Right faction would prevail. However, the threat from the Left was always distinct.

'You're out of order, delegate! Please resume your seat!' This was the penalty for those who failed to observe protocol.

Now, with the final day underway, Steve Kavanagh turned to

the next item on the agenda. A special resolution on 'Financial Control'. Unusual, but he'd noted it. Proposed by General Secretary of Allied Rural Industries Wal Newell. The proposer would supply supporting documents at the time of his address.

'The National Conference calls Delegate Wal Newell to the microphone!'

The delegate duly stepped up, clutching a brief of papers.

'Comrades,' he began, 'I have the sad duty to reveal to you a tragic tale of financial betrayal, perpetrated at the highest level.'

There was a collective intake of breath.

'Yes, I will shortly table this brief of material, obtained by assiduous research, in which I was helped by those sympathetic to achieving fiscal responsibility – and ensuring the highest standards of probity.'

'Get to the point, delegate!'

Holding aloft one paper after the other, Wal Newell would do just that.

'I will. Sheet one details a secret money account held in the Cayman Islands, the start of this financial deceit. It runs into the millions. Sheet two is a letter signed by the account holder authorising special withdrawals from Treasury to set up such an account. Sheet three gives the details of multiple deposits during the last several years, with a long addendum covering several pages, detailing the advantages of that tax haven, with assurance of non-extradition. Finally, details of shell companies fraudulently set up. Sheet four is a photocopy of plane tickets booked to the Caymans for either a holiday there or, more likely, criminal flight.'

'Shame, shame!'

'Yes, and sheet five details various real estate brochures from the same tax refuge, far from any possible extradition to Australia! The account holder intends to live it up there. What do you think, comrades? A life of wine, women and song. All on us!'

'Who owns the account?' The uproar was starting.

Facing towards the Chair, Wal Newell's finger pointed to the alleged culprit.

'Prime Minister Bob Hawke! Comrades, I demand you depose him right now!'

Bob Hawke was flabbergasted, his jaw open. He didn't see this coming. He knew Wal Newell was from the far left, along with Allied Rural Industries. But this was way out of line. Leaping to his feet, the prime minister was now incandescent with rage.

'It's not me. I'm innocent! This is a monumental stitch-up!'

Indeed it was.

Walking over to the Chair, Newell tabled the documents. 'Mr Chairman, I table these before I make a further proposal.'

Steve Kavanagh had to bang his gavel for a full five minutes before the uproar subsided to a tolerable level. The members of federal caucus and cabinet were shocked to the core.

The whole time, Bob Hawke kept shaking his head.

'Delegate Newell, we'll have to check these documents to verify their authenticity. However, they appear detailed.' They certainly were. The Stasi forgers had created a veritable masterpiece. 'In the meantime, you may provisionally make a proposal. What is it?'

'Thank you, Chairman. In the light of this gross fiscal turpitude, I propose Prime Minister Hawke step down immediately and be replaced by a wholly more responsible member, present here. A man of undoubted probity, who has many others in parliament behind him.'

Turning to a delegate seated close by, Newell beamed. 'The member for Mainwaring, Ern Rickard!'

The uproar resumed.

Bob Hawke flung his papers onto the floor, his many comments unheard in the din. Then Steve Kavanagh resumed control.

'Delegates, this is spectacularly out of order. For one thing, it is a long-established principle that choosing a leader is not the prerogative of the National Conference. In any case, both we and the Australian Federal Police will have to examine the purported veracity of the documents tabled.'

Bob Hawke kept shaking his head. 'I've never been to the Caymans in my life and won't start now!'

'However, I'll allow the motion to be discussed on one condition – we look at its second part before deposing the prime minster. That is, the suitability of the alternative candidate, Ern Rickard. We may well ask, how qualified is he?'

Bob Hawke, though puzzled, seemed slightly more comfortable now.

Both Wal Newell and Ern Rickard were somewhat taken aback. The chairman continued.

'The honourable member for Mainwaring migrated from Bamberg in West Germany some years ago to Perth, became active in the Australian Labor Party – that much is clear – changed his name from Richter to Rickard – nothing wrong with that – and, with a change of nationality to Australian, was then elected to federal parliament, as you know. So far, so good.'

'What's your point, Chairman?' Ern Rickard couldn't help himself.

'Just one thing, Delegate Rickard. You're ineligible to become prime minister or even stay in parliament! I have here papers proving you failed to properly renounce your German citizenship when you assumed Australian nationality. The Constitution clearly states...'

Now it was Ern Rickard's turn to be shocked. Also Wal Newell's. Their planned coup had collapsed dramatically.

How did Kavanagh know all that?

'Delegate Rickard. I suggest you resign from parliament immediately and fix up your citizenship matter. Don't worry, you can stand again in 1990!'

Nineteen ninety! They had entirely different plans for that year.

Now it was Bob Hawke's turn to show relief. What a set-up. Those papers had to be forged.

Furious, Wal Newell looked at Rickard and cursed his carelessness. The Stasi minders would sort him out, well and truly, for on such a vital mission, failure is never accepted. Otherwise, heads will roll. By being in on the plot, his own head was on the chopping block, too. He'd go out in style. Oh, he had one last ace to play, in the event of mission failure, which could be used to level the score as well.

Death to capitalists!

Newell ripped something from his pocket and rushed forward. 'I'll fix you, Hawke!'

'Watch out, Bob!' Steve Kavanagh reacted first, flinging up his arm to protect the prime minister.

The threatening object fell to the floor. Pumped with adrenaline, Hawke was onto Newell, thumping him a mighty blow to the jaw.

Whack!

'Cop that, you dingo!'

Newell collapsed and, before he could think about it, had two security men pinning him to the floor.

'Don't touch what he had – some sort of weapon.'

Exactly right, straight out of the Stasi dirty tricks file. A vial of a deadly nerve agent. Pressed against someone's nostrils – well, it would be good night. Used either to kill an opponent or as a suicide weapon to avoid capture.

Newell had failed on both counts.

Many rushed up to console Bob Hawke and express sympathy. The female minutes secretary included. Not one to overlook a pretty face, Bob smiled.

'Don't put all this in the minutes, love. They'll never believe it!'

In the hubbub, Ern Rickard eluded security by slipping away. They would detain him soon, hiding elsewhere in the venue, knowing he was just as involved as Newell. But for now, he had time to find an office phone and make a last call. He got straight through with the shocking news.

Curse that document he'd failed to check. Yes, renounce German nationality! How did they know he'd forgotten that?

The hated capitalists had more brainpower than he thought.

CHAPTER THIRTY-TWO

Scrambling aboard the Ansett Airlines flight, which had been delayed at least ten minutes on her behalf, Lillian gratefully collapsed into her allocated seat. She was lucky she'd escaped a drenching from the incoming deep low which was now pummelling the coastline.

Guilty over knowing she alone had been the cause of the plane's delay, she smiled nervously at the passengers who met her gaze. The detective sergeant needn't have worried, as most of them were more interested in their reading matter or the worsening weather outside, supposing meteorological reasons to have delayed the flight.

'My appointments,' she whispered to the attentive flight attendant, who took the parcel of her revolver and handcuffs for safekeeping during the flight, as protocol dictated.

When the aircraft eventually reached cruising speed, Lillian could at last relax and plan what she'd do upon reaching Coffs Harbour, the short flight taking less than an hour. Klaus Ziegler had a good start on her and was no doubt holed up either in the basement of Allied Rural Industries headquarters in Vernon Street or some other hideaway.

What would the spy do next? Looking for inspiration, she glanced outside.

'Wow, this weather is a shocker. It's really throwing it down outside!' It certainly was, the small aircraft being buffeted by the huge storm it was flying into. Well, that was one obstacle she'd have to cope with. For another, hopefully the rental car would be ready on her arrival, and she'd be able to track him down before he was able to complete what he intended to do.

'Fasten seatbelts, all passengers! Prepare for landing!'

The usual instruction was rather shriller than normal, thanks to the continual tossing this way and that. This would be a white-knuckle landing.

Indeed it was, with three attempts to ground the aircraft, dangerously blown around almost as though it was a balsa wood model, before, with engines revving, it was safely on terra firma and idling its way towards the terminal. Relief all round. They couldn't resist clapping to acknowledge the pilot's evident skill.

'Double his salary, Sir Reg!' one wag called out, to loud laughter. Would the airline's founder, Sir Reginald, do that? Fat chance.

Waiting till the others had departed, Lillian reclaimed her appointments and quickly made her way off the plane to the car rental desk.

'Vehicle booked for Lillian Boyd, please. I phoned through from Sydney.'

'Certainly, Ms Boyd. A Holden Monaro sedan. Please sign here.' It would suit her fine.

First stop, Allied Rural Industries. She'd brought with her the latest car phone – a veritable brick. Just before she departed the parking lot, there was an incoming call.

'Detective Sergeant, there's a report of a veritable fracas at the ALP National Conference in Hobart. Two foreign agents detained. One tried to kill the prime minister!'

'What!'

'Don't worry, Hawke's OK. Gave a good account of himself, from all reports. The Hobart Australian Federal Police are interviewing both of them as I speak. D'you reckon there's a third one still on the loose?'

'I don't reckon, I know! I'm on his trail right now.'

'Good luck. Let us know if you want backup.'

'I will. Thanks.'

No, this one had become personal. In her mind was emblazoned the image of poor Ursula dying in the gutter, left without mercy. If not for that young Sophie, there wouldn't have been a clue. Nothing would bring back Ursula, but by the grace of God, she might be able to stop further damage.

Skidding in the wet conditions, she revved the Monaro a little too much as she accelerated towards Vernon Street. She had a definite idea what that damned spy was up to.

She prayed she'd be in time.

Driving his stolen vehicle through the night, Klaus Ziegler made every effort to stick to the road rules, especially the speed limit, as he headed northwards. The last thing he needed was police attention.

His comrades knew their mission in Hobart well. And if Hawke was deposed and replaced as prime minister by Ern Rickard, the honourable member for Mainwaring, it would mean an entirely new regime for Australia. He could see it now!

'The Socialist Republic of Australia!'

Sure, there would be constitutional difficulties in the way, and it wouldn't happen overnight, but the process would begin. In fact, the SRA could wait for a decade or so, but the important – indeed, the essential – target was to renounce the US alliance and tilt towards the Soviet Union, which could begin almost at once. Backed by left-wing unions orchestrated by Wal Newell, they'd be heading towards that goal very soon. And Ern was just as vital.

'Yes, plenty of left-wing MPs are in his pocket. Victory will be ours!'

Ziegler loved his self-talk, knowing Wal and Ern had played their part. Once Hawke was out, they'd get going.

Arriving at the Coffs union headquarters, he was pleased all staff had been given time off, thanks to the National Conference. They'd be working overtime once it finished to implement the various decisions made. The place was deserted.

He parked in the basement – all the better to conceal the stolen car in case there was a search for it by now. He had no further use for it. The rest of his plan would be accomplished with the utility left for him by careful arrangement, recently serviced with a full fuel tank. Not that he'd have to drive far.

Yes, exactly as he'd asked, there was what he'd need. Just as planned, the signal lantern. Especially powerful, with a high beam. He tested it, and it worked perfectly, lighting up the basement. Bright as day. You'd see it for kilometres.

Ziegler knew the code, having been briefed some time back by the Stasi. Three flashes for 'yes' and one for 'no'.

Oh, he felt it in his bones. He'd be giving three flashes to change the course of history. He needed to rest after his night drive but would be ready once darkness fell.

'Tonight's the night!'

Then the bottom dropped out of his world. Equipped with his own car phone, he took his first call, putting his ear to the 'brick'. Ern Rickard was on the line, frantic.

'Comrade, all is lost. We failed in Hobart! Hawke survived. Abort the mission. Security is coming for me–'

The line went dead.

'What! How did those cretins muck it up? It should have been foolproof!' he yelled, then restrained himself. He wasn't going to stop, nonetheless. He, Klaus Ziegler, didn't give up, and he didn't fail. He knew exactly what to do.

He'd force the issue. There was still a chance.

How long till it was dark?

He checked his watch. Fortunately, in early winter, night fell early, especially in gloomy, stormy weather. Not so long to wait.

Once he'd taken charge and completed his role, he'd find refuge somewhere. Maybe get to the embassy in Canberra and be smuggled out of the country. At least his part of the mission would succeed, and those two idiots could rot in an Australian jail forever. He'd safeguard his own reputation.

Ziegler lifted the lantern into the back of the ute and covered it with the tarpaulin provided – not that rain would worry it. Going up to the office, he was just about to raid the fridge and help himself to a much-needed dose of hard liquor when he heard something outside.

What was that Holden Monaro doing?

Someone was at the front door. Some woman, and she looked official. A cop? His sixth sense told him she was trouble. Fortunately, everything was locked up, with a notice on the door indicating headquarters were closed for the duration of the conference.

Still, she hung around. Ziegler fingered his firearm. If need be, he'd dispatch her. It was too late to back out now. He moved to where he'd have a clear shot through a slightly ajar window. He checked the silencer.

'Nosy woman, your last moment has come...'

She moved away, clearly convinced there was nobody there.

Ziegler smiled and relaxed. He could enjoy the bottle of spirits undisturbed, as he heard the Monaro start up and pull away from the kerb. He was fine.

Fortune was smiling on him, and he poured himself a double dose. Then another.

Outside, the heavens opened. The storm, which had briefly relented, now resumed with added fury.

This was going to be a low weather system to remember.

CHAPTER THIRTY-THREE

Lillian certainly knew what Klaus Ziegler was likely to do but was unsure of the exact timing. It could be tonight or sometime soon. There was one way to estimate when. She drove through the cyclonic conditions to Coffs Harbour Police Station, a welcome respite from the continual rain starting to flood the streets and the increasingly violent storm.

Provided with a comforting meal from the canteen, she obtained the latest data from Marine Surveillance's Coastwatch. Here was an eighth position of the mysterious offshore ship. Her calculations told her that if it held its present course, which it was extremely likely to do, the vessel – yes, identified as a Soviet battle cruiser – would be exactly offshore by 8 p.m. that night, she estimated between four and five kilometres off a certain location.

'They've got a hide!' Lillian exclaimed to a constable bringing her a comforting cup of strong coffee. 'That's deep within Australian waters. Whatever happened to the twenty-kilometre coastal limit?'

'I'd say you're onto something, Detective Sergeant. Do you want backup?'

'No, Constable, this is personal. It's been a long story, starting with a hit-and-run in Randwick one Melbourne Cup Day. This one's down to me.'

On a stormy day in June, with darkness ready to close in, this could easily be a decision Lillian would deeply regret.

That afternoon, there was excitement on board the *Kalinin*, steaming towards the New South Wales coast. Once they received the prearranged signal of three flashes from their agent onshore, precisely at 2000 hours, they would have confirmation to proceed southwards to Sydney Harbour and triumphantly enter it on an impromptu goodwill visit.

They anticipated that after a few days of welcoming selected guests on board the Kalinin, newly installed Australian leader Ern Rickard would be primed to officially acknowledge the ship's groundbreaking arrival. His next official act would be to invite Admiral Rostov and senior officers, accompanied by Horst Moltke and Otto Dreschner, to a special reception at Kirribilli House. This magnificent home and estate overlooking the harbour, next to the equally stunning Admiralty House, was the prime minister's Sydney residence.

'Comrades, we can begin planning our takeover of the country that very day, as we walk around the grounds.' Admiral Rostov and the two Stasi heads were ebullient. Already, Moltke and Dreschner were jockeying for position. One gave the other a knowing wink. 'The GDR will be a leader in Europe after this comes off!'

They helped themselves to shots of vodka from Rostov's cupboard, merely at the thought of their coming victory.

Rostov continued, 'Rickard can ram some changes through. The left-wing unions and members of the Australian parliament will be emboldened to proceed further down the road to socialism. Cancel the ANZUS alliance with the Americans and eject the US bases. Goodbye to Pine Gap and North West Cape. Unless the Soviet Union takes them over!'

'It will be a new world order!'

'Despite the weather, let's all be on deck at 2000 hours for the signal. Then it will be full steam ahead to Sydney Harbour. Comrades, call your valets and get your best suits pressed in the laundry. Get ready for your first sight of Sydney Harbour and their much-vaunted opera house. We'll get them to play a merry tune.'

Outside, the storm raged and crashed, the *Kalinin* tossed so severely by the waves it was hard to maintain the correct course. The weather system's ferocity was unparalleled, its fury relentless. Going outside would require a heroic feat of strength, but if they huddled inside, they'd miss the eight o'clock signal.

No way would they miss it!

Suddenly disquieted by the storm's intensity, Otto Dreschner had a disturbing thought.

It couldn't be an omen, could it?

CHAPTER THIRTY-FOUR

Lillian knew the time and now had to estimate the location. A quick drive around and a town map consultation gave her the likely spot – the southern break wall at the end of Jordan Esplanade. The break wall would give an offshore vessel, even on a night as stormy as this one, a clear line of sight.

She parked the Monaro some distance away, zipped up her storm gear and reconnoitred the area. She noticed a utility parked nearby, not a vehicle that meant anything to her in itself. It might be significant. Or nothing.

Now, at 7.50 p.m. with the weather even worse, she noticed the local council had put up barriers with notices as clear as anything despite the general lack of visibility. 'Danger No Entry – Break Wall Access Closed.' That was obvious. Well done, Health and Safety. She stepped around them.

The feel of her Smith and Wesson on her hip gave Lillian some comfort. She needed it, with the rain pelting down. A glance at the noisy, roiling ocean waves smashing against the break wall meant going further wouldn't be for the faint-hearted.

She uttered a quiet prayer. The cyclonic rain drenched her as the ocean raged in response, even worse than before.

There was no sign of him. Lillian fervently hoped she hadn't got the location wrong. Whatever he was about to do, she'd have to prevent it.

She was comforted by another glance at the town map, wrapped in waterproof plastic. The end of Jordan Esplanade had to be the spot. She slowly advanced towards the very tip, just as the storm was reaching its climax, with huge waves crashing over the top of the break wall, wetting her legs and threatening to wash her away. Undaunted, she went on.

'Got him!'

With her watch showing mere seconds to 8 p.m., in front of her was a shadowy figure, the outline of a large apparatus before him. He was eagerly watching the horizon. In the storm and winter gloom, it was impossible to see anything out there.

That hardly worried the man, who was suffering the same threat from the giant waves.

Then she saw it. A huge beam from the apparatus lit up the gloom, directed seawards.

A searchlight – he was signalling! Just as she suspected.

Seconds later, kilometres offshore, there was an answering signal.

She had to stop him!

'Police! Klaus Ziegler, put your hands up! Now!'

He didn't.

Almost skidding in the cascading surf around him, the German drew his gun, shooting at Lillian. Instinctively, she ducked, and the bullet ricocheted off the rocks, screaming into the distance. Despite the imminently threatening surf, she drew her service revolver and returned fire, also missing her target.

In desperation, Ziegler lunged for the signal lantern, intent on two more flashes. This cursed cop wouldn't stop him.

Lillian drew a bead on it. Two bullets crashed into it, shattering the glass. It was useless.

She was momentarily vulnerable. Ziegler had an infinitesimally brief opportunity to level the score. She was in his sights, too slow to bring up her Smith and Wesson. Half a second and...

Thump!

Just as he was about to squeeze the trigger, a gigantic wave burst over the break wall and engulfed him. His firearm lost, he was instantly washed over the edge and into the maelstrom below.

'Noooo!' was the only sound from Klaus Ziegler's lips as he was gripped by the massive force of nature, sucked down into the roiling ocean, then smashed into the rocks of the barrier before returning to the depths, totally beyond human help.

A victim of the worst storm to pound Australia's east coast that winter, the spy's body was never found.

'Help! Help!'

The same wave almost engulfed Lillian Boyd.

Her fingernails breaking and her own firearm swept away, the detective sergeant just managed to cling to the rocks, barely keeping herself out of the unforgiving ocean's clutches. Thoroughly exhausted, one more wave would finish her, and she'd suffer the same fate. She was resigned to ending up in Davy Jones's locker...

'Hang on, lady! We're coming! Don't let go!'

She didn't.

Cec Aitken and Barry Howard hadn't been happy when rostered by Coffs Harbour Council to be on patrol that freezing winter night, 'just in case'. The town clerk was a stickler for occupational health and safety and was concerned people would disregard the warning signs to keep away from the break wall in a storm. Instructed to keep a close watch out, the council employees had noticed the two figures ignoring the warning sign shortly before and hurried to the location. Bravely, they put aside the very real threat to their own safety once they realised the emergency. Cec and Barry were armed with a long rope, once again 'just in case'. One chance only. Desperately, they tossed it.

'Grab it, lady!'

She did, just as she was engulfed by another wave, her grip on the slippery rocks lost. Falling, with the deadly waves unwilling to release her from their eager clutches, Lillian was dragged down into the freezing ocean with just enough presence of mind to hold her breath as she went under, resurfaced then went under again. She clung to the rope, her one and only lifeline, like a woman possessed.

'Help!' she screamed, on briefly resurfacing, as she noticed one of the men had lost his grip and fallen over, at risk of joining her in the raging ocean. The other held on grimly, bracing himself against a large rock. If he gave way, all was lost...

Then, with the deadly ocean currents relenting for an instant, the fallen man regained his footing. Both men braced themselves, summoned every ounce of strength and slowly, gradually reeled her in to safety over the rocks, oblivious to any bumps or scratches. Her strength utterly spent, a grateful Lillian collapsed into their arms, clutching both her rescuers for dear life as the trio appeared transfixed there like an artist's tableau.

It must have been half a minute till she could summon up just enough energy to spit out a mouthful of seawater and speak.

'Thanks, thanks, you wonderful blokes, but can you get me off this damned death-trap and back to solid ground?'

'We sure will, lady. But next time, show some common sense and don't come out here in a storm!'

'Don't worry. There won't be a next time!'

Amen to that.

- - -

Cec and Barry were worried about Lillian getting hypothermia because of her immersion in the freezing water, so hurried her back to their temporary base, a demountable a short distance away. Wrapping her in a blanket, they boiled a jug to make coffee. In answer to their obvious question as to why she'd been there, she just answered 'police business'. They didn't enquire further.

As her condition improved, Barry comforted her while Cec went back out on patrol in case anyone else was 'stupid enough to go out on the break wall'.

'Yes,' Barry began, 'you wouldn't know, but I was tempted to take a sickie tonight because of the foul conditions. I thought nobody would go out on the break wall in this storm. But my old dad, Morry – he's a widower and lives with the wife and me – is a stickler for the rules. Knowing how I was thinking, he told me to do my duty. Even so, I was still tempted.'

'I can understand that,' Lillian interrupted. 'You wouldn't expect anyone out there.'

'I know, I know. Then he told me he'd had a message from God – he's got religious in his old age. *"Barry, I think you're going to save someone tonight!"* What do you make of that?'

'Well, it's true, so it must have been from a higher power!'

'Yep, that's typical of the old man. Straight as a die. A retired watchmaker – ran Howard's Watches for years here in Coffs. The old bloke had a hard life. Barely survived the war in Europe over forty years ago. Locked up in a concentration camp, would you believe? Then became a reffo – sorry, refugee – from Germany after the war. Changed his original names to Morry Howard to make them more Australian, but kept the same initials. I suppose others did that, too.'

'I guess so. Anyway, I'm in your debt, and Cec's. Also your dad's, indirectly. Please thank him for his "message". And now it's time to phone the local cops to collect me. I'm not in a fit state to drive. Got your brick handy?'

Barry found it and dialled the number. What a blessing – a 1980s-era mobile phone.

As she waited, Lillian struggled to recall an old story from her childhood. No, it couldn't be. What were the chances? When everything settled down, she'd turn her detective's brain to another very simple piece of research. She may have one more visit to make in Coffs…

Offshore, those on the *Kalinin* were initially cheered by seeing the first flash, with the ship signaller responding. As the ocean raged, the storm beat down and the battle cruiser tossed up and down in the tempest, they waited in vain for any further flashes.

For them, no further signal. What they had received was clear. There was no invitation to dock in Sydney Harbour. The coup must have failed.

How could it, after such careful planning?

The Stasi doesn't fail!

They waited for what seemed like hours but was only minutes. Lashed with rain, Admiral Rostov and the two Stasi heads retreated inside, defeated by the frustrating darkness. There was nothing further from the Australian coast. Despondent, the radio operator got the admiral's attention. He'd picked up a radio station ashore.

'A great National Conference. In fact, a beauty!' Prime Minister Bob Hawke was ecstatic. 'Yes, we had a bit of argy-bargy, but we expected that. You might say I gave as good as I got! Nothing we couldn't handle. So now, we go on with our program and plan for 1990, an important year. Yes, 1990. Mark it in your diaries! Why so? As you have already heard, by 1990, no Australian child will–'

Stepping up to the microphone, Rostov barked, 'Captain, alter course for an immediate return to base in Vladivostok. We're wasting our time here!'

Rostov looked straight at Moltke and Dreschner. 'Comrades, return to your cabins. You're a pair of incompetents. I don't want to see either of you again before we reach port. German efficiency, my eye!' To emphasise the point, he snatched away the vodka bottle they were hoping to empty in celebration.

Crestfallen, they had no answer. He went on…

'Wait till the Kremlin gets my report. You can choke on your cursed Democratic Republic! I hope you're both for the high jump! I'd make the noose myself, if I could!'

It would be a long, sad voyage back to port. Especially for Rostov. Gorbachev would be furious once the truth came out. They'd gone behind his back! The ruthless admiral hadn't counted on failure – he'd imagined only the glory of success, seeing himself as the next general secretary of his much-loved, all-powerful Soviet Union, a world leader if he'd pulled this one off, steaming into Sydney Harbour for the glory of communism... But now, he'd be cashiered for sure. If not worse.

A very sad return voyage indeed.

EPILOGUE

The rot had set into the German Democratic Republic years before the audacious Operation Southern Cross was launched. On their long trip back to East Berlin, Moltke and Dreschner had ample time to reflect on where their repressive regime had gone wrong. Running a network of spies to harass their own people and conduct operations against politically free nations was the worst of it. But there was more.

Much more.

There'd been a coffee crisis in the latter seventies, with a huge price levy imposed for importing that popular drink. East Germany habitually lacked hard currency. The regime was forced to add a range of fillers, highly unpalatable.

Though this crisis eventually passed, it proved there were basic economic problems in running a state along communist lines. Their rationale was structurally unsound, and this would have wider implications.

Huge debts were owed to Western institutions, and East Germany lacked the capacity to export goods of quality to the West. Thus, the debt grew. With much of the budget allocated to the Stasi, a useless expense in itself, the situation only worsened.

'Comrade,' Moltke reflected to Dreschner during the unpleasant voyage back to Vladivostok, during which the two were wracked by seasickness on an unforgiving ocean, 'I suggest we do what we claimed Hawke had done. Set up accounts in the Cayman Islands. Shell companies with a false trail. A buffer for when it all goes belly-up...'

Dreschner didn't know what to think. An extraordinary suggestion from a committed communist. But he warmed to the idea.

'Yes, sir, let's do that. I'll get the boiler room working on it as soon as we're back. A happy retirement fund, you may say.'

Of course. Look after number one!

He hoped Moltke being immediately seasick as he spoke wasn't an omen.

Human greed? Always trumps any political system.

On docking back in Vladivostok, Admiral Rostov, hoping to save his own skin, lodged his report of mission failure the moment the two East Germans were put on their plane back to East Berlin, via Moscow. As predicted, the Kremlin was in an uproar.

The admiral was fired on the spot, retiring in ignominy. Gorbachev was furious at being deceived about the true nature of the *Kalinin*'s voyage. Not to mention the expense of the naval program.

'A hundred billion roubles, and this is all we get! Chernenko must have been mad to approve it! Forget any idea of mastering the Pacific – leave it to the Yanks!'

The general secretary, as history would record, was bent on liberalising the Soviet regime but still wanted to keep the Soviet Union together. However, it would be all downhill for the USSR from then on. He gritted his teeth for the party's reaction.

Outspent on both defensive and offensive weapons by the West, the Soviet Union was gradually going broke. Its communist government, which had no effective answer to a free enterprise system, finally collapsed in 1991. The USSR dissolved, freeing those republics which had been forced under its control. To his credit, Gorbachev refused to use force to keep his realm unified. They could go their own way, which horrified the hardliners.

Three, conquered years before by a ruthless Josef Stalin – Lithuania, Latvia and Estonia – were especially grateful. Others could set their own course.

Russia itself would have a new regime. For better or for worse? Time would tell. Yet for now, freedom tasted wonderful!

- - -

Steve Kavanagh continued to have a distinguished career in journalism, earning an award for his initiative in researching the background of 'Ern Rickard', acting on his gut reaction about the 'honourable member'. His contact in Immigration had worked through the night to find him what he needed.

Steve also earned Bob Hawke's undying gratitude for his quick reflex action in deflecting the would-be assassin's arm. His nickname, 'Lightning Fast', endures to this day.

As for spies Ernst Richter and Walter Neumann, they provided to ASIO valuable intelligence information about the Stasi in exchange for a reduced prison sentence. They were eventually deported, only to face further justice in West Germany.

Klaus Ziegler's master's degree, largely plagiarised, was expunged from the University of Sydney's records. Kendrick Findlay had to write an interesting explanatory report to his department's director. His golf games were put on hold for a month.

Mikhail Gorbachev was the last General Secretary of the Soviet Union, although this was never his intention. The whirlwind of change he unleashed broke apart the USSR but ushered in an era that could have led to democracy for his people. It was no criticism of his efforts that, sadly, such proved not to be the case. He resigned in late 1991. A later effort to re-enter politics was entirely unsuccessful. His reforms had been lauded throughout the West but were far less popular at home.

After Rostov's failed, unauthorised mission of 1988, the Soviet leader phoned Bob Hawke to apologise, once all the facts were evident. After giving a full explanation with great embarrassment, he was heartened by the prime minister's reply, 'No worries, Gorby, I sorted it out! She's all apples now!'

The puzzled general secretary needed to make a special phone call to the Australian Embassy in Moscow to get that interpreted. Only then could he relax.

Mikhail Gorbachev lived to be ninety-one, dying in August 2022. He left the legacy of ending the Cold War and changing Europe forever – for the better.

Bob Hawke would go on to win his final election in 1990 but by July of that year confronted a wholly different challenge from the events of June 1988. Australia was in severe recession. The prime minister's popularity declined with the country's financial fortunes. In the ensuing instability, Bob Hawke was replaced by Paul Keating in December 1991. An inglorious end to a long prime ministership. He did, however, achieve the role of elder statesman and never lost the affection of the Australian people, dying at the age of eighty-nine in May 2019.

Gregor Laube, forced as a disciplinary measure into a non-combat role, finished his national service without having to shoot at any more would-be escapees. He then followed the lead of his mentor, Pastor Kasner, into the Lutheran Church ministry, serving God faithfully throughout his country.

By 1988, along with other Protestant churches, he encouraged the growing wave of opposition against the state and advocated liberalisation, playing an effective part. Pastor Laube called for 'society with a human face'. However, though he had married happily years before, he never won the heart of young Angela.

She, as Angela Merkel, later became the first woman chancellor of a united Germany, a position she filled with distinction over a long period. In later years, Gregor Laube had the privilege of visiting her in Berlin as part of a Lutheran delegation to discuss the plight of refugees settling in Germany. There was a gleam in her eye as she recognised in him the eager young man who had sought to win her affections. Their meeting was extremely cordial.

Xanthe Young recovered from her failed romance with Klaus Ziegler, later marrying a work colleague. On learning of the Stasi spy's background in a confidential report, she congratulated herself on her narrow escape. She gave her parents wonderful birthday presents by way of thanks.

Parents often know best!

Lillian Boyd, fresh from a valour award bestowed by the NSW Police Commissioner in the proud presence of her superior, Inspector Chris O'Rourke, took a period of leave, although not before calling to see Jonas Schneider. Stressing the espionage information was strictly confidential, she told him the hit-and-run case was closed, with the guilty party now beyond earthly justice.

'So poor Ursula's death had a purpose after all! Had he not hit and killed her, we might never have known what he was up to... that's some consolation.'

'Yes, Mr Schneider. Please hold onto that!'

He did.

Afterwards, she travelled straight up to Katoomba, where her parents still lived. Spending time with them and enjoying the mountains again was just what she needed.

As she drove, she thought back to their early life in Australia, some of it too early for her to remember. Her brother, James, had a slightly better recollection.

Yes, after arriving in Sydney as 'ten-pound Poms' on the *Arcadia* in the autumn of 1952, they had gone straight to Bradfield Migrant Hostel for several weeks' orientation. By the end of that, her mum Annabelle's parents had provided a loan for their first and only business – Summit Books, which they set up in the Blue Mountains. Hard work and enterprise paid off, and the bookstore became a chain throughout mountain towns in New South Wales, Victoria and Tasmania. Now, with their recent retirement, the business had passed to James, who had plans to develop the franchise further.

As well as a happy reunion with them, she had a small favour to ask.

Looking slightly more stooped than the last time she'd seen him, her dad, Ben Fletcher, was still spry enough at seventy-one, as he opened the front door to greet her.

'Come in, sweetie! Mum will put the kettle on. Great to see you again.'

As they embraced her, Ben and Annabelle couldn't wait to hear her latest news about the valour award. They were as proud as punch about how Lillian had turned out. She was one of a kind, that daughter.

Getting right down to it after their affectionate greetings, Lillian came out with her request.

'I've already told you about the cold case I've now solved?'

They nodded as she reminded them about poor Ursula Schneider.

'Well, it would be great to promote her children's books in our business – sorry, James's business now. I'll urge him to go for it. Let's hope *Great Gertie Goanna* and *Elusive Edrick Echidna* live on...'

Ben was definite. 'James will, if I have anything to do with it!'

Annabelle agreed.

'Good, because her illustrator was able to complete the last unfinished one, and it's right for printing. Summit can now sell the whole series. Jonas Schneider will get the royalties for life.'

'Don't worry, you've got a decent brother. Consider it done!'

Ben was eager to get to the award. 'So, fill us in about the medal you got. I realise it was all hush-hush, but tell us what you can... Don't tell me it was East Germany again!'

'Sadly, they were still the snake in the grass. You wouldn't believe it!'

So the tale unfolded with no significant detail omitted. Then, her personal climax – her miraculous rescue at the hands of the two council employees, whose names she told them.

'Dad, does Barry's father's name – Morry Howard – mean anything?'

'No, should it?'

'It wouldn't, of course. How about his former name?' And she produced a letter, showing her dad the signature with Morry's original name in brackets. You could hear the cogs whirr before the penny dropped. Poor Ben was astounded.

'Moshe Horwitz! Who would have thought? What a blast from the past!' He sat down to read, as his eyes misted over. Soon, he was crying openly, as Annabelle and Lillian comforted him. 'To think it was his son who saved you! What a coincidence!'

They both looked at him.

'No, of course it was no coincidence. I thank God that was how He arranged it. If Morry – Moshe – felt he was in my debt, it's now been repaid – in full.'

'What do you reckon, Dad? Do I see a reunion trip to Coffs Harbour coming up?'

Lillian smiled as she thought of her final visit in Coffs once her official report was done, and the welcome she'd received from old Morry once he realised who she was. He'd treated her to copious cups of coffee while he put pen to paper, pouring out his gratitude to Ben for his action over forty years ago.

Ben stood up to embrace Lillian again, then winced as he sat down. He didn't let it stop him from doing anything, but his old wound would sometimes trouble him when the weather changed. He thanked God for his one remaining kidney.

It was as sound as a bell.

- - -

Lillian's grandmother, Myrtle, visited her family three times over the years, and they had more than one trip back to England, a country Lillian and James had no memory of.

It was during her last visit to Katoomba that Myrtle quietly passed away in her sleep. Her Bible by her bedside, she had a look of utter contentment on her face. She lies buried in the local cemetery.

Hermione and Horace Kingsley both lived happily to old age. In the former's case, it was one hundred and two years, becoming a grand old lady who loved her horses. At their funerals, St Giles Church was filled to overflowing, acknowledging for each a life well-lived.

Horace would have been delighted with the coded message accompanying the wreath on his casket. British Military Intelligence never forgot him.

The prediction Ben had made about the new queen, Elizabeth II, as he and his young family were sailing away from Britain that cold February day in 1952, came to pass. The longest-serving monarch in British history, Queen Elizabeth's highly successful seventy-year reign ended only in September 2022, following her death at age ninety-six. A stunning achievement by any measure.

Following the Queen's model, Ben and Annabelle also both passed away in advanced years, happy in the knowledge their full lives were completed. Greatly loved by James, Lillian, other family members, their church congregation and the Katoomba community, they were entirely contented.

In East Germany, things went from bad to worse.

Despite a reinforced border, citizens were still managing to escape to the West. The centrally planned economy, state-owned, failed to respond to economic circumstances. In addition, the government was forced to pay substantial war reparations to the Soviets. For its part, Australia was unimpressed by the GDR once the full report on Stasi activities was received and closed its embassy in East Berlin. Likewise the Canberra one.

By mid-1989, the situation was at crisis point. A rigged GDR election was held, increasing the number of citizens either applying for exit visas or leaving illegally. Thousands managed to escape to the West via Hungary, which removed its border restrictions with Austria. There were mass demonstrations against the regime.

Nevertheless, state leaders celebrated the fortieth anniversary of the GDR in October.

The popular rising couldn't be quelled, and with the cruel regime weakening and essentially rudderless, large crowds gathered at checkpoints near the Berlin Wall. Unprepared and indecisive, guards faced the prospect of being forced to let them through. All they needed was the signal from the collapsing state.

Watching his television set in a dismal frame of mind, one resident of the Sunset Lodge Nursing Home on the outskirts of East Berlin was appalled by these developments. He couldn't understand them. What were people thinking? Just then, his nurse Trudi Hegel entered, bringing his dinner on a tray.

'Pumpkin soup, then a little roast beef. Sorry the rations aren't better. It's all the upset outside doing it. The state's about to collapse...'

'What do you think, Trudi?' He was utterly confused.

'Well, I've resigned. You'll have a substitute nurse from tomorrow. The moment the wall's opened, I'm heading west! If you want to know, that's what I think!'

'What!'

'Yes! But before I go, I need to say something. You don't know who I really am, of course. Hegel is my married name, but I was born Trudi Rittmeyer. Does that name mean anything? My father was Oskar Rittmeyer.'

The old man searched the recesses of his mind before he remembered.

'Of course. I, er, interrogated him. It was my job, you know.'

'You did, Mr Schwarz, and as far as it being your job, you gave him a terrible time. Five years' jail almost broke him, but he survived and had some good years before he died. At least I had a father for some of my adolescence. He did forgive you and was grateful that, at least, you spared his life. So I, too, forgive you. I just want you to know that before I go. Goodbye!'

With that, Trudi turned and left. He could just see her scampering through the breach in the wall, along with thousands of others, at the first opportunity.

Reinhard Schwarz, prematurely aged in his late seventies, hardly touched his dinner. He'd been a bereft man ever since the news of his much-loved only nephew Klaus's death had come through the year before. Drowned so far away in the service of the great German Democratic Republic. He'd aimed so high.

Poor Klaus Ziegler, his sister Helga's only child – she and Erich would mourn him forever. Reinhard had ensured the boy would live up to the highest communist ideals. His own career with the state had come to naught, but he'd had hopes for Klaus. Now dashed. Life was pointless. What would poor Helga do?

Continuing to stare at the commotion on the screen, the euphoric citizens exulting at their imminent freedom, Reinhard felt only disgust and a gut-wrenching sense of betrayal.

Had it come to this?

He pushed his tray away at the very moment the eager citizens surged through the gap in the wall, others grabbing sledgehammers to start demolishing the hated barricade.

November 9, 1989. The Berlin Wall fell at last. Freedom was in sight!

On that very night, Reinhard Schwarz, alone in his room, collapsed and died from a massive heart attack. With his beloved regime having vanished, he had nothing left to live for. He never got to meet the substitute nurse.

In a move that would have horrified him, in March 1990, East Germany held its first free elections, but it was all too late. Following negotiations with West Germany, the laws of the East were to be replaced by those of the Federal Republic. On October 3, 1990, the two halves of Germany were united, including both East and West Berlin.

East Germany officially ceased to exist.

On the day prior to this cataclysmic event, Horst Moltke fled to Moscow in a bid to elude justice, his goal of establishing a refuge in the Cayman Islands having come to nothing.

Otto Dreschner and family prepared to do the same. However, the former directorate head had one last phone call to make, to his astrologer.

'You promised me 1990 would be a watershed year, with today's date circled. A famous date, one I'd never forget. October 3. I've given years of my life for Code 1990. Do you hear me? Code 1990! What do you have to say for yourself?'

'Well, it proved to be exactly that, didn't it? A momentous day!'

'Yes, but...'

'If you don't like our predictions, then don't trust astrologers!'

At least that was good advice.

As for the former repressive, Stalinist state of East Germany, it ended right where it had always deserved.

Consigned to the dustbin of history.

Stasi headquarters

Stasi files

Prison cells

Prime Minister R.J.L. Hawke

East Germany's emblem

M. Gorbachev on the move

A glance at freedom

Road to Pine Gap Northern Territory

ACKNOWLEDGEMENTS

With deep gratitude, I firstly acknowledge those who encouraged me to continue writing, following my previous publication of three books of fictional stories. This time, *Code 1990* is clearly a novel based on certain actual events, involving both known and invented characters, with some of the themes taken from an earlier unpublished novel I wrote in the mid-1970s.

Secondly, I acknowledge family, friends and readers in my own community who asked what would come next with my author journey. After three books produced in reasonably quick succession, there was the expectation of more to follow and I trust this one won't disappoint. Léonie, as before, generously gave me computer time when the writing bug struck. She also became invested in one particular personality in the story so I had to be careful how that played out. I thank our adult children for their various acts of encouragement, especially those who read through the entire story to give their observations on both characters and plot.

Thirdly, special mention is due to a friend who wishes to remain anonymous for her quick reading of the first draft of the manuscript and her perceptive comments, given in much detail. She was indeed generous with her time and talents. As well, regional librarian Debbie Campbell (Local Studies and Digitisation) gave me very helpful background detail of Coffs

Harbour that's an integral part of the story and, with a site visit, I was able to place this in the context of the plot. I also wish to acknowledge the assistance of IT guru Denis Church for the historical photos included, sourced and adapted thanks to his skill and persistence. These should bring home to the reader exactly what happened when those well-remembered events unfolded.

Finally, I am extremely grateful for my committed editor, Teri Kempe, herself a gifted author with considerable publishing experience, for her usual incisive, valuable advice. I thank Teri for her very timely input.

ABOUT THE AUTHOR

Apart from times overseas, Ray Keipert lived in various Sydney suburbs prior to retiring north with his wife Léonie in 2013. After joining his local University of the Third Age writers' group, Ray was motivated to write short stories and poems, contributing to the group's book publication project. A number of his short stories have received awards in literary competitions, including second place in one hundred and forty-eight entries.

In 2020 Ray co-published an edition of twenty fictional short stories, *Life's Winners... and a Few Losers*, followed by the 2021 publication of five longer stories in *Five in the Quiver*. Some of these were sequels to events and characters in his first book. In 2023, he published *A Hand of Aces*, two novellas in the one volume.

Inspired by the lure of creative writing, Ray continues to plan and prepare further books.